Poppy raised the collar of her coat and shoved her hands into the pockets. Taking a steadying breath, she cocked her head. "What is it you want?"

He wants me. She fought a surge of pleasure at the thought, a pleasure that sharply spiked when Ben pulled her to him.

"I'd like—" he paused and a slight smile lifted his lips "—to know if you have plans for the rest of the evening?"

"I—I do," Poppy finally managed to stammer.

"I wasn't aware you were seeing anyone." An emotion she couldn't identify flickered in the molten silver of his eyes. "Who is he?"

"Rocky." Her grin came quick and fast, surprising them both. "Rocky Road."

He chuckled, a low, pleasant rumbling sound, his gaze lingering on her lips. "Have dinner with me. Rocky can wait."

ONE NIGHT WITH THE DOCTOR

BY
CINDY KIRK

MILLS & BOON

First published in Great Britain 2013
by Mills & Boon, an imprint of Harlequin (UK) Limited,
Eton House, 18-24 Paradise Road, Richmond, Surrey TW9 1SR

© Cynthia Rutledge 2013

ISBN: 978 0 263 90154 2
ebook ISBN: 978 1 472 00546 5

23-1013

Harlequin (UK) policy is to use papers that are natural, renewable and recyclable products and made from wood grown in sustainable forests. The logging and manufacturing processes conform to the legal environmental regulations of the country of origin.

Printed and bound in Spain
by Blackprint CPI, Barcelona

Cindy Kirk has loved to read for as long as she can remember. In first grade she received an award for reading one hundred books. As she grew up, summers were her favorite time of year. Nothing beat going to the library, then coming home and curling up in front of the window air conditioner with a good book. Often the novels she read would spur ideas, and she'd make up her own story (always with a happy ending). When she'd go to bed at night, instead of counting sheep she'd make up more stories in her head. Since selling her first story to Mills & Boon in 1999, Cindy has been forced to juggle her love of reading with her passion for creating stories of her own...but she doesn't mind. Writing for the Cherish™ series is a dream come true. She only hopes you have as much fun reading her books as she has writing them!

Cindy invites you to visit her website, www.cindykirk. com.

To my three favorite girls: Wendy, Grace and Hannah.
You brighten my world every day.

Chapter One

Golden beams of light shone through the windows of the two-story house situated in the mountains overlooking Jackson Hole. Although Christmas had been a month earlier, garlands of greenery and wreaths with plaid ribbons still adorned the large wraparound porch.

Poppy Westover added her serviceable Ford to the dozens of cars already parked in the clearing east of the house. Tiny snowflakes danced across the well-scooped path as she began the trek to the front steps of the house she'd passed only moments before. Ducking her head, she forged onward. The brisk north wind slapped her cheeks and ruffled her hair.

Lights might illuminate the walkway, but the dark of the winter evening still closed in around her. By now, the party had been going on for an hour, almost two. She prided herself on being timely, but a last-minute call to secure an emergency foster placement had delayed her leaving the office.

Poppy reached the steps of the beautifully decorated

porch just as a sleek black Mercedes drove slowly past. *Another late arrival.* The thought that she wouldn't be the last to show up buoyed her spirits even as she grimaced at the familiar lines of the vehicle.

Though this was a newer version and a different color, a similar CL550 coupe had been her ex-husband's pride and joy. Even with public transportation readily available, he'd insisted on driving the car to social functions. And there had been lots of such events. As a prominent Manhattan neurosurgeon, Bill Stanhope had been on everyone's must-invite list.

Poppy had grown increasingly weary of socializing with his associates and people he'd wanted to impress. People who lived an extravagant and loose lifestyle; married men and women who took lovers as easily as another glass of champagne.

This evening would be different. Tonight she'd be among people who shared her values. Friends. Former schoolmates.

Dr. Travis Fisher, the host of the party, had graduated from Jackson Hole High with her. Back in the day, they'd even dated briefly. Now he was married, the father of five and one of the top ob-gyns in Jackson Hole.

Poppy rang the bell then jammed gloved hands into her coat pockets and hunched her shoulders against the wind. Thankfully she didn't have to wait long. The door opened and a flood of warmth and delicious smells spilled out.

Frowning at her chattering teeth, Travis motioned her inside and shut the door firmly against the winter chill. An efficient young woman dressed all in black offered to take Poppy's coat.

After shrugging off the soft cashmere, Poppy murmured her thanks then held both hands out to Travis. "Thanks for inviting me."

"We were determined to hound you until you accepted one of our invitations." He gave her fingers a firm squeeze and coupled the gesture with a warm smile. There was something intrinsically likable about the tall doctor with sandy-colored hair.

"You look lovely this evening," she heard him add.

Poppy glanced down. She'd dressed in such a hurry that for a second she didn't recall what she'd pulled from the closet. Though she knew most women used the party as an excuse to wear something new they'd gotten for Christmas, this year her family had sent money rather than gifts.

Unfortunately her new job kept her far too busy for shopping. Because of that, she'd been forced to call into service a red cashmere turtleneck dress from several seasons back and last year's black-heeled boots.

The dress had been purchased the first year after her divorce. Her ex considered bold colors "gauche."

Poppy smoothed her hand against the ruby-colored cashmere. The fabric molded against her body, gently hugging her curves. Stylish. Feminine. *Gauche.* She smiled. "I'd never have worn something like this back in high school."

She'd been preppy then. Seriously preppy. Plaid jackets. Diamond pattern sweaters. Pearls. How she'd loved those pearls.

As if remembering his own questionable fashion sense during those years, Travis grinned. "Those were good years. Good times."

When his smile slipped Poppy remembered Travis's parents had been killed at the end of his senior year, leaving him in charge of his seven siblings. Yes, she mused, looking too far back probably wasn't advisable. For him. Or for her.

Travis placed a hand on her elbow and guided her through a foyer rich with the scent of evergreens. They stopped at the edge of a large room where elegant women in stylish dresses mingled with men in dress pants and sport coats.

The star at the top of an enormous, brightly lit Christmas tree winked on and off as if pulsing in time to some unheard tune. A cheerful fire crackled noisily in the hearth of a massive stone fireplace. Conversation and laughter wafted pleasantly in the air. Poppy exhaled a breath and the tension in her shoulders eased.

"I heard you scored a job with social services." Travis's eyes held a look of admiration. "They're lucky to have you."

"I'm the lucky one." Poppy adored children. The opportunity to help foster kids, while challenging, had been a dream come true.

The melodious chimes of the doorbell sounded and Travis cocked his head. A rueful smile touched his lips.

"You'll have to excuse me," he said smoothly, giving her arm a gentle squeeze. "I'm on door duty."

The other late arrival, Poppy thought.

"Tend to your guests." She waved to several women across the room. "I'm in the mood to mingle."

Travis took several steps then turned back and called over his shoulder. "Check out the mistletoe."

Mistletoe? For a second she was puzzled. Christmas had been a month ago. Then Poppy remembered the retro party the Fishers had hosted last fall, right after she'd returned to Jackson Hole. Tiny sprigs of little red berries and shiny green leaves were everywhere.

When she'd asked, someone told her that mistletoe had been a big part of Mary Karen and Travis's courtship and they hung it at every party.

Taking Travis's words as a warning, Poppy glanced up, trying to spot any troublesome berries or waxy leaves. There might have been one in the beamed ceiling but she couldn't be sure.

A delicious aroma of cinnamon mingled with evergreen while the hum of conversation and laughter wrapped around her shoulders like a favorite sweater. Her lips lifted. Poppy had been invited to several Christmas parties but had declined all offers. She wished now that she'd accepted.

"Poppy," Mary Karen Fisher shrieked, rushing over. "I'm so happy you made it."

The intensity and underlying warmth of the greeting

made Poppy smile. She chatted easily with Travis's petite, pretty wife who looked adorable in a sapphire blue tunic dress, her blond hair falling in a mass of curls past her shoulders.

When one of the catering staff asked for a moment of Mary Karen's time, Poppy meandered over to the tree. It was real, she realized with a start of pleasure, fingering the soft needles of the fir, inhaling the intoxicating scent.

She'd been much too busy to put her own tree up this year. If there had been someone to see it, Poppy might have gone to the effort. But her mom and dad had remained in California for the holidays. They lived in Sacramento now, just down the block from Poppy's sister and brother-in-law and their three children.

Knowing this would be their oldest daughter's first Christmas since she'd relocated to Jackson Hole, her parents had offered to make the trip to Wyoming. But Poppy knew how much they'd been looking forward to seeing Aimee's children open presents on Christmas morning. If her dad were here, he couldn't dress up as Santa for the grandkids, like he'd done for her and Aimee.

Poppy had seen no option but to inject a hint of regret into her tone and tell them she'd already made plans to celebrate the holidays with friends.

Her parents' relief had been almost palpable. They believed her, of course. After all, she'd always had a wide circle of friends.

Poppy's mouth lifted in a wry twist. For as long as she could remember she'd been the pretty, popular older sister. Yet, it was Aimee who now had what Poppy had always wanted: a fulfilling life that included not only a rewarding career but a loving husband and children.

When Poppy had married eight years ago, she'd been certain it would last forever. Never had she imagined that her husband would cheat on her. Or that she'd be divorced, childless and starting over at thirty-four.

"I almost didn't recognize you," a deep voice murmured.

An involuntary shiver slid up her spine at the sound of the rich baritone. She snagged a glass of champagne from a passing waiter's silver tray before turning to meet Dr. Benedict Campbell's steely gray eyes.

As usual, the man looked positively delectable. Tonight he wore brown trousers, a cream-colored button-down shirt open at the collar and shiny Italian loafers. His razor-cut dark hair was short enough to be professional but long enough to tempt a woman to run her fingers through the chestnut strands to see if they were as silky as they looked.

Benedict was an orthopedic surgeon and a darn good one if public opinion could be believed. He was also one of the most eligible bachelors in Jackson Hole. They'd chatted briefly on several occasions. While he'd always been pleasant, she'd done her best to avoid him whenever possible. Goodness knows she'd had enough of arrogant doctors to last this lifetime.

He touched a strand of her dark hair. "This is different."

"I got it cut yesterday." She quenched the sudden urge to pull back from his touch. "I wanted to go even shorter but the stylist told me to try it to the shoulders with a few layers first. She said I could always come back and have more cut off."

Poppy pressed her lips together to stop her nervous chatter.

"It suits you," he said easily as if they were discussing nothing more personal than the current weather forecast. Yet when his eyes met hers, she saw pure masculine appreciation in the liquid depths.

Lifting his glass of wine he tapped the crystal against hers. "To being adventurous."

She hesitated. Though his smile was smooth, his expression bland, she sensed an undercurrent of challenge. As she hesitated, he raised a brow. Deciding she was being silly, Poppy took a sip.

They stood there for several heartbeats, gazing over the sea of people. She told herself to make an excuse and walk away but the testosterone wafting off him kept her tethered where she stood.

If anything, she had to fight the urge to lean into him. What had her mother always said? *Stand too close to the fire and you'll get burned.*

"Travis warned me about the mistletoe." She blurted the first thing that came to her mind when the silence lengthened.

Benedict's lips quirked upward. "I'm surprised he said anything. Both he and Mary Karen seem to take great joy in watching their friends get caught under those tiny sprigs."

"Seems kind of foolish to me," Poppy mumbled, then immediately wished she could pull the words back. Just because she had no intention of making a public spectacle of herself didn't mean other people might not enjoy an unexpected kiss.

Killjoy. Isn't that what her ex had once called her when she'd complained about the endless parties? Hadn't he made it clear the reason she wasn't having fun at the events was because of her attitude? Perhaps he'd been right.

"It's much too early in the evening for a sigh." Benedict's eyes turned sharp and assessing.

Poppy could feel her face warm. "I—"

"Why yes, I'd love to dance." He took her hand and grinned. "Thanks for asking."

She almost told him this was a cocktail party, not one of those fancy affairs at the Spring Gulch Country Club. Until she saw a space had been cleared in the middle of the room and more than one couple was swaying to the music from the big band era piped in from overhead.

They reached the edge of the impromptu dance floor before she could protest. When he pulled her to him and they began to move in time to the smooth tune, it was difficult to remember why she'd hesitated. His arms were strong and sure, one hand settling on her waist, the other holding hers in a firm grip.

Poppy told herself that once this song concluded, she'd make an excuse and get as far away from Benedict as possible. For now, dancing was preferable to making small talk. Except when they were simply talking, she hadn't been quite so aware of his broad chest or the strength in his arms. And she hadn't realized just how good he smelled.

The scent, spicy with a hint of tang, tickled Poppy's nose in a very pleasant way and made her want to press close to get a bigger whiff.

A female vocalist was singing about the glories of love. Poppy resisted the urge to snort. She'd once been an incurable romantic, a hopeless optimist, a love-struck fool. She was older now. Wiser.

Then what the heck are you doing in Benedict's arms having a good time?

Red warning flags began popping up in her head.

"How do you like your new job?" he asked in a low tone, his warm breath tickling the top of her ear.

"It's very rewarding." She made the mistake of glancing up, meeting those magnificent eyes framed by thick eyebrows and incredibly long lashes.

There was something in the slate-colored depths that made her stumble. A heat she hadn't expected. Nor had she expected an answering desire to course through her veins like slick, warm honey.

Feeling more than a bit panicky, she tried to recall what she knew about the man who held her so confidently in his arms. Benedict was dating a fellow doctor. That's right. He wasn't interested in her. He was simply being polite. She let her shoulders relax. "How's Mitzi?"

Okay, so perhaps she could have been a little more subtle, done a better job transitioning into the topic. But darn it, keeping a clear head was difficult when she was breathing in the intoxicating scent of his cologne mixed with the clean fresh smell of soap.

He cocked his head. "Mitzi Sanchez?"

She gave a jerky nod.

"She's fine." He looked perplexed. "But why ask me?"

"Because you're dating." Poppy spoke almost primly. "It's polite to inquire about a person's significant other."

He laughed then, a booming laugh that caused the couple dancing next to them to turn and smile.

"Mitzi and I are friends, colleagues." Benedict dropped a hand to her arm then steered her to an area where it was less crowded so they could talk. If he noticed the stiffening in her spine, he didn't mention it. "We haven't dated in months."

Poppy wondered if Bill had explained her away so easily to all the women he'd seen when they were married. "I saw the two of you together at The Coffee Pot only a couple of weeks ago."

At Benedict's puzzled look, she continued, filling in the blanks.

"It was a Sunday morning. You were seated beside her." Poppy lifted her chin. "I saw you," she repeated.

His expression turned thoughtful. "Large table? Back of the room?"

"That's correct," she said hesitantly now, wishing she could think of a way to change the subject.

All the attention he was giving the matter caused a knot to form in the pit of Poppy's stomach. Too late she realized her error. She'd made him think that somehow it mattered to her if he was dating Dr. Sanchez. When it didn't. Not at all.

"There's a group that meets at The Coffee Pot every week after church." His eyes filled with understanding. "I can see where you might have gotten the wrong impression."

"Forget I said anything." Poppy waved an airy hand. "You don't owe me an explanation."

"But I do," he murmured.

Startled, she widened her eyes. "Why?"

"Because I want to kiss you." Benedict trailed a finger down her cheek. "It wouldn't be right to do that if I were involved with someone. Or if you were. Are you seeing anyone, Poppy?"

"Me?" Her voice rose then cracked. "No. I'm not seeing anyone. What's this about kissing? You can't—"

"Look up," was all he said.

Poppy lifted her gaze. Directly above her head hung a sprig of shiny dark green leaves. Her heart stuttered. "Mistletoe."

The word barely made it past her lips when his mouth was on hers. She didn't know a whole lot about mistletoe other than it seemed that most who found themselves under the leaves settled for a peck on the cheek. Apparently Benedict hadn't gotten that memo.

The kiss started out sweet. His lips were firm and warm as they molded against hers. Just when she expected him to pull away, his tongue swept across her lips and she'd opened her mouth to him before she realized what she was doing.

By then it was too late. Desire, hot and insistent, filled her veins. Her arms wound around his neck and she pulled him closer. By the time the kiss ended, her breath came in short puffs and her body ached for more.

She took a step back, feeling his gaze on her. Poppy resisted the urge to straighten her dress and smooth her hair. Instead she placed a polite smile on her lips, mumbled something about needing to speak with someone across the room…and bolted.

Chapter Two

Poppy ignored him the rest of the evening.

From across the room Benedict watched the pretty brunette laughing with Lexi Delacourt, a fellow social worker. Even though Poppy had a clear line of vision to him, she didn't once glance in his direction.

Benedict rocked back on his heels and blew out a breath.

"Perfect Poppy is hot." Tripp Randall, the CEO of Jackson Hole Hospital, spoke over Benedict's left shoulder.

"Perfect Poppy?" Benedict raised a brow.

"That's what everyone called her back in high school."

"Why?"

"Always looked perfect, I guess." Tripp shrugged. "You should go after her."

"Save your breath, Randall." The smile he sent the administrator showed a lot of teeth. "I don't need a matchmaker."

Still, Benedict understood the hopeful undertone. Tripp obviously found it encouraging that he was showing interest in Poppy, rather than Tripp's younger sister, Hailey. The fact that he and Hailey had gone out on several dates in the past six months hadn't sat well with the hospital administrator.

Though Tripp considered him a friend, heck they even played on the same basketball league, he was protective of Hailey and believed that, at twenty-six, she was much too young for him.

Benedict didn't agree with that assessment but he didn't care enough to argue the point.

"That was some kiss you shared under the mistletoe," Tripp continued in an offhand tone that Benedict guessed was anything but casual.

"So good—" Benedict pulled his gaze from Poppy and frowned "—she hasn't spoken to me since."

He had to resist the urge to turn back to Poppy, to keep her in sight. But that would make him look desperate, which he most certainly had never been and wasn't now.

"How odd." Tripp brought a glass of champagne to his lips. "From where I stood earlier it appeared she enjoyed locking lips with you."

Benedict lifted a shoulder in a slight shrug and studied the dark burgundy liquid in his glass. Poppy's reaction after the kiss puzzled him, as well. He was positive, or *almost* positive, he hadn't misread the interested signals she'd been giving off.

It wasn't as if they'd been strangers. He'd originally met Poppy last fall at another of Travis Fisher's parties. Benedict had enjoyed their brief conversation that night. Enjoyed it so much he found himself hoping their paths would cross again at one of the parties over the holidays. She hadn't shown her face at any of the events. Until tonight.

Although he'd arrived late, the moment he spotted Poppy he was glad he'd come. It had been going well until he'd stolen a quick kiss with all the finesse of a schoolboy in the throes of a first crush.

Benedict raked a hand through his hair and expelled a

harsh breath. He had no one to blame for the current situation but himself.

"Why don't you ask her to dance again?"

"Why don't you mind your own damn business?" Benedict shot back, frustration twisting his gut into a knot.

"Okay, okay." Tripp raised his hands, palms out.

The sound of feminine laughter rang out and Benedict slanted a quick glance in Poppy's direction. God, she was beautiful. The red dress hugged her body like a second skin.

"Want to hit the Flying Crane with me?"

Benedict jerked his attention back to Tripp.

"On the fourteenth." The hospital administrator's eyes took on a hopeful gleam.

"That's Valentine's Day," Benedict reminded him. "I'm pretty sure you don't want to spend the evening with me when you could be with her."

He gestured with his head to where Tripp's bride stood speaking with the hostess. Adrianna, or Anna as she'd recently instructed him to call her, was lean and voluptuous with thick dark hair and a face that belonged on a cover of a fashion magazine. She was also a well-respected midwife.

Tripp shifted his gaze and Benedict experienced a stab of envy at the pride and love in the newly married man's eyes.

"Anna will be at the Crane participating in a Torch Singing competition that night." Tripp snatched a canapé from a passing waiter's silver tray. "It's a fund-raiser for Community Safety Net."

"A worthy cause." It was impossible to live in Jackson Hole and not be aware of all the good work being done by the nonprofit. The organization provided shelter and advocacy to victims of domestic violence and sexual assault.

"I thought you might want to come and help me cheer her on," Tripp added.

Since he wasn't dating anyone special, Benedict hadn't given much thought to Valentine's Day. He supposed spending an hour or so at the popular bar knocking back a couple of beers with Tripp while watching Anna sing could be fun. "What exactly is torch singing?"

Tripp hesitated. His face took on a pained expression. "The contestants sing sentimental love songs—"

The words came more quickly at Benedict's snort of laughter.

"—with a distinctly jazz and blues influence."

"I'll check my calendar," Benedict told him. "If it turns out I can't make it, tell Anna I'll happily make a donation."

"Coward."

Benedict laughed. He sobered when he saw Winn Ferris swagger over to speak with Poppy and Lexi. His gut tightened as Lexi sauntered off, leaving Poppy alone with the man.

Last summer, Winn had blown into Jackson Hole as an emissary of GPG. His employer, a large investment firm based in Atlanta, had deep pockets and a mission to develop every inch of Jackson Hole.

Although Winn pushed and pushed hard, his golf course project had gotten hung up in the environmentally sensitive guidelines passed by the county several years earlier. Those who expected Winn to give up and return to Georgia with his tail between his legs had been mistaken. He'd stayed and continued to fight.

Benedict liked the business executive, had found him to be intelligent with a good sense of humor. But Winn wasn't the right guy for Poppy. She needed someone different, someone more…grounded in Jackson Hole.

Out of the corner of his eye, he saw her flash Winn a brilliant smile. When Winn responded by looping a friendly arm around her shoulders, a knife twisted in Benedict's gut. Though he'd planned to stay and enjoy the evening, Ben had the feeling if he didn't walk away now he might do something stupid. Like tell Winn to back the hell off.

With frustration fueling his steps, Benedict was halfway across the room when Poppy's eyes met his. He told himself to just keep walking. But something inside him locked into place at the connection.

She held his gaze long enough for him to see the heat shimmering in those beautiful green eyes. Heat directed not at Winn Ferris, but at him. Then Winn touched her arm and Poppy shifted her gaze back to the business executive.

Yet there was no denying for that one instant there'd been a tangible connection between him and Poppy. Benedict found himself whistling as he walked out the door.

Over the next two weeks, Benedict's thoughts strayed to Poppy at odd times. But he didn't have a chance to do more than wonder how she was doing. A rash of skiing and motor vehicle accidents had kept his surgical schedule full.

After finishing an emergency open reduction of a comminuted tibia fracture, Benedict left the hospital to return to his office. He still had to see the handful of patients who'd chosen to wait, rather than reschedule. To his surprise, he discovered that one of his associates, Dr. Mitzi Sanchez, had stayed to help him out.

By the time the last patient limped out the door, even the receptionist had gone home. Apparently most of the staff had plans for Valentine's Day.

Other than me, he thought. *And Mitzi.*

He and his beautiful colleague had once been involved. Now they were simply friends.

Benedict sat behind his desk and dictated a letter back to a primary care physician thanking him for a referral. So many surgeries in the past fourteen days had left him behind on such paperwork. Since he didn't have anything going this evening, he told himself it would be a good opportunity to get caught up.

"Tell me you're not hanging around here all night."

Benedict recognized Mitzi's voice and a jolt of uneasiness swept through him. He hoped she wasn't on the verge of suggesting they go out for dinner or something equally crazy.

"Your concern about my social life warms my heart." He kept his tone light and his eyes focused on the monitor.

"What's the matter, Ben? Couldn't find a date?"

He heard a hint of laughter in Mitzi's tone as well as the familiar bite.

Finally glancing toward her, Ben noticed she'd exchanged her white lab coat and work clothes for a dress that hugged her curves and reminded him of stretchy silver lace. High heels in the same color showed off slender legs. He didn't blink an eye when he noticed her hair. Instead of the color of honey streaked with caramel as it had been yesterday, it was now a rich dark walnut.

He narrowed his gaze even as relief flooded him. There was no way she'd gotten herself all dolled up for *him*. "Who's the lucky guy?"

Her full lips lifted. "Kelvin Reid."

Ben had treated the NFL linebacker several months earlier when he'd been injured in a skiing accident while vacationing in Jackson Hole. "Proximal humerus fracture with dislocation."

Mitzi chuckled. "Kelvin will be happy to know you remembered him so personally."

Pushing back his chair, Benedict stood, but remained behind his desk. "I didn't realize the two of you were friendly."

"We chatted several times when he came into the office to see you," she said with a studied nonchalance deserving of an Academy Award.

"If he came back to take you out on Valentine's Day, you must have hit it off."

"What can I say?" She drew up one shoulder in a slight shrug. "Men find me irresistible. Unless, of course, we're talking about you."

"Mitz," he began.

"Don't look at me like that." Her eyes held an impish gleam. "I'm over you every bit as much as you're over me."

"That's good to know," he said in a dry tone that made her chuckle.

"But you are my friend." She fluffed her hair with her fingers. "That's why I stayed late to help see patients. By the way, you're welcome."

Though he'd already expressed his appreciation to her earlier, he smiled. "Thank you, again."

"You know, Ben—" she brought a manicured finger to her mouth, tapped it against her lips "—you should check out the Torch Singing competition tonight at the Flying Crane."

"Thanks for the offer, Mitz." He spread his hands on the desk and leaned forward. "But I have no desire to spend the night with you and your new boyfriend. That would be awkward for all concerned."

"Well, for starters, Kelvin is my friend, not my *boy*friend. And I didn't invite you to spend the evening with us. Kelvin and I have dinner reservations at the Gun Barrel," Mitzi said, referring to a place known for their mesquite grilled steaks and wild game. "You'll like the atmosphere at the Flying Crane. Trust me."

"I've been there before," Benedict informed her. "It's a nice enough place, but I'm not really in the mood to listen to a bunch of schmaltzy love songs."

"Even if Poppy Westover is singing?"

Feeling the weight of Mitzi's assessing gaze, Benedict deliberately kept his expression bland. "Anna Randall is also competing. Tripp asked me to go with him to support Community Safety Net. I turned him down."

Mitzi pointed to the phone on his desk. "Tell him you've changed your mind."

"Why would I want to do that?" he drawled, even as he considered the possibility.

"Because you want to do your duty and support this important fund-raiser." Mitzi's brightly painted lips lifted in a Cheshire cat smile. "Why else?"

* * *

Poppy gazed into the dressing table mirror and added a touch of gloss to her cherry red lips. A stranger stared back at her. Cassidy Kaye, the backstage stylist and former high school classmate, had arranged Poppy's hair into a "top reverse roll." Poppy had been apprehensive but had to admit the pompadour-like style suited her face. And she decided the two bright sparkly pins that winked back at her—one from above her temple, the other just behind her ear—added a festive touch.

Her dress, a 1940s era floral sheath, nipped in at the waist and fell just below her knees. Bending over, Poppy adjusted the seams of her stockings then lifted to straighten the strand of red beads encircling her neck.

"You're up next." The balding stage manager with a walrus mustache motioned Poppy forward. "Break a leg."

Offering the man a shaky smile, Poppy smoothed suddenly sweaty palms on the skirt of her dress. What had she been thinking when she agreed to participate?

Granted, she loved to sing. That was the reason she'd joined the church choir. In fact, it had been after one of the evening rehearsals when Lexi had ambushed—er, pulled her aside—and innocently asked if she wanted to volunteer for a Jaycee fund-raiser. Being civic-minded, Poppy had immediately said yes. When she learned what she'd agreed to do, she'd considered pulling out. It had been years since she'd set foot on a stage.

How could she possibly perform with only a few weeks to pick her song and practice? But then, she reminded herself to stop setting impossibly high standards. The performance didn't need to be flawless or perfectly choreographed. This was a fund-raiser, not a Broadway musical.

From where Poppy stood just offstage she could see that not only were all the tables full, there were people standing in the back. Of course, she reminded herself, more people meant that a community organization, which did a lot of good, could do even more.

When she heard the applause for Anna Randall and saw the midwife take a bow, Poppy's stomach quivered. Adrenalin mixed with a healthy dose of fear surged. In less than a minute she'd be the one standing under that spotlight.

She reminded herself that the only person she might disappoint tonight was herself. Unlike most of her fellow contestants, Poppy didn't have anyone in the audience who'd come specifically to hear her.

"Please put your hands together for Poppy Westover." David Wahl, an emergency medicine physician and emcee for the evening's event, held out his hand to her.

Poppy took a deep breath and strode onto the stage to a smattering of applause. She glanced over the crowd and froze. The man whose torrid kiss had never been far from her thoughts the past two weeks sat at a small table in the front row.

Benedict saw the look of startled surprise in her green eyes before she looked away.

"She's happy to see you," Tripp observed, then took a sip of beer. His lips twitched.

Shock was closer to the word that had come to Benedict's mind. Had he been mistaken about the desire he'd seen in her eyes two weeks ago as he'd left the party? Still, she didn't look angry. That was some consolation. Though he now had to wonder if the gesture he'd made before leaving the office had been a smart move.

Since it was too late to change anything now, Benedict took a pull from the bottle of Dos Equis and sat back, ready to enjoy the show.

It took only a few notes for Benedict to realize that Poppy had a voice suited to this style of singing, warm with a bluesy richness. As the song continued he leaned forward, mesmerized.

She drew out the final note and the crowd rose to their

feet. Cheering filled the bar. Even as he clapped, Benedict turned to Tripp. "She's as good as any professional."

"Poppy had the lead in several musicals when we were in school. She's even better now." Tripp shook his head. "I can't imagine anyone topping that performance."

The words barely registered. Benedict's entire focus remained on the stage. He gave Poppy a thumbs-up and she blushed.

When Poppy bowed one last time, Benedict didn't take his eyes off her. He'd been given a second chance to make an impression.

This time he wouldn't blow it.

Chapter Three

After her performance, Poppy headed straight to the dressing room. She reached the small table with her name written on a strip of paper taped to the mirror and came to an abrupt halt. The makeup brushes littering the tabletop had been pushed aside. In their place sat a crystal vase holding a dozen long-stemmed burgundy roses.

She brought a hand to her breast and glanced around. "Are—are these for me?"

Although she'd spoken to no one in particular, Cassidy Kaye, owner of the Clippety Do-Dah salon, looked up from the supplies and brushes she'd been stuffing into an oversize purple bag.

The silver sparkles in Cassidy's atomic blue eyeshadow glittered in the artificial light. "And you told me you weren't dating anyone." Her shocking pink lips curved up in a smug tilt. "You had to know I'd find out."

Like a fine wine, some people got better with time. Others, well… Poppy sighed. The hairstylist was just as nosy as she'd been back in high school when she'd written the Loose Lips gossip column.

Dressed in skintight purple pants and a bright emerald green sweater, Cass still marched to her own beat. Her blond hair, jagged to her shoulders, currently held a streak of fuchsia. Canary yellow glasses were tipped up at the corners and studded with rhinestones.

Even when she'd been small, Cassidy had exhibited a bold, eclectic and totally unpredictable fashion sense. In kindergarten, she'd regularly worn a Halloween catsuit to school in lieu of more traditional attire. In sixth grade she'd come to school with her hair buzzed, demanding they call her Sinead.

Not everyone had been kind to her.

Remembering, Poppy felt her irritation ebb. She reached out, rubbing a soft, fragrant petal between her fingers. How long had it been since anyone had sent her flowers? Years, she decided.

She wished these beautiful blossoms were hers. But she'd learned long ago wishing didn't change reality.

"I bet these were simply placed on the wrong table." Regret filled Poppy's voice.

"The flowers are yours." Cassidy's chin lifted. "I was here when they were delivered."

Poppy widened her eyes at the stylist's defensive tone. "I didn't mean to imply—"

"See." Cassidy plucked a card from the bouquet and shoved it under Poppy's nose. "Your name is right here."

Conscious of the curious glances from the other contestants now directed her way, Poppy took the envelope from the stylist and glanced down. Her name in elegant cursive stared back at her.

Unable to contain a shiver of anticipation, Poppy broke the seal with one finger and slowly pulled out the card nestled inside.

"Break a leg" had been scrawled in bold masculine strokes followed by a single name, "Ben."

The warmth that rushed through her was chased by a prickle of alarm. *Doctor* Benedict Campbell wasn't someone she wanted to notice her, much less buy her flowers.

Cassidy jostled close, rising on tiptoes to peer over her shoulder.

Biting back annoyance at the woman's obvious attempt to see what was on the card, Poppy casually dropped it into her purse. The last thing she wanted was for rumors to get started about her and Benedict.

"Who sent them?" Poppy demanded.

"A friend." Poppy's tone came out light and breezy, just as she'd intended.

"Puh-leeze." The stylist rolled her eyes and emitted a braying laugh. "I'm not stupid."

"It happens to be the truth. Regardless of what you may think, Be—" Poppy stopped and cleared her throat. "The man who sent the flowers is merely a friend. Really a friend of a friend. Actually, more of an acquaintance."

Cassidy hooted and glanced meaningfully around the room, but found herself playing to a dwindling audience. Without an immediate answer the other contestants had quickly lost interest in the "who sent the roses" game.

"A guy would never send something that pricey to a woman he considered an acquaintance or even a friend." The stylist spoke loudly. "A gesture like that has lover written all over it."

Out of the corner of her eye, Poppy saw Anna Randall cast a sympathetic glance in her direction. Anna had gone to school with her and Cassidy and was well aware of the stylist's predilection for drama.

Poppy retrieved the cardboard carrier and the cellophane the florist had left next to the dressing table. Although she knew better, she clung to the hope Cassidy would give up the snooping and wander off. But when she looked up, the woman was still there.

Cassidy tapped a finger against her lips. "A dozen long-stemmed set this guy back plenty," she said as if thinking aloud. "Florists jack up the prices something fierce around Valentine's Day."

Poppy simply shrugged and pretended to check her makeup. As she leaned close to the mirror, rose petals—soft as cashmere—caressed her cheek.

Now that the bouquet was up close and personal, Poppy realized that, unlike some of the inbred varieties, these roses possessed a wonderful scent, sweet without being cloying. Giving in to impulse, she buried her face in the fragrant blossoms and inhaled deeply.

"Give me a hint," Cassidy said the second Poppy lifted her head. Apparently deciding to go with the subtle approach, the stylist used a persuasive tone that invited confidences. "Who is your mystery man, Poppy? Do I know him?"

Poppy was spared the need to respond when she and the other contestants were called back to the stage. After considerable fanfare, David Wahl announced she was the winner of the competition. Poppy stared in stunned disbelief when he pressed a small silver microphone trophy into her hand and presented her with a check for $50. She kept the trophy but promptly donated the money to Community Safety Net.

The crowd cheered loudly. As she glanced over the enthusiastic throng, Benedict, er, Ben, gave her another thumbs-up and she offered him a smile, not a flirty one but the kind you'd give your grandmother or the helpful stranger next door.

But when his eyes held hers an instant longer than comfortable, friendly didn't begin to describe the jolt. Poppy realized with a twinge of alarm that she wanted this man. Not in her life, oh most certainly not there, but in her bed.

It was a startling revelation. She'd had many opportunities for trysts since her divorce, but no interest. It was as if her desire for sex had died when she discovered her husband had been unfaithful for most of their married life.

Now, one smoldering look from Benedict had stirred those embers. No, not just stirred. The spark in those gray eyes had ignited a bonfire hot enough to paint the sky in bold red strokes.

Being blindsided by this unexpected desire didn't change the fact that, for Poppy, sex had always followed love. And Benedict wasn't the kind of man she would allow herself to love.

Once bitten…

There was one more round of applause for all the contestants before they were ushered off the stage. She told herself not to look but Poppy couldn't help it. She cast a quick glance in the doctor's direction.

He was gone.

She shoved aside something that felt an awful lot like disappointment. It was a blessing, she assured herself. Always best to have temptation out of reach.

Once she reached the dressing room Poppy scooped up the roses along with her purse, trying to block the other contestants' excited chatter about their evening activities.

She wasn't sure why she suddenly felt blue. After all, it wasn't as if she didn't have plans. Exciting plans that included a bowl of ice cream and a favorite DVD.

After declining a last-minute offer to have a drink with Cassidy and a group of her friends, Poppy slipped out the back door, telling herself quite firmly that Colin Firth on screen would have to do. Rolling around on the sheets with Benedict wasn't an option. Not tonight. Not any night.

Though for a moment, the thought of a spontaneous night of pure fun made her heart quicken.

With fear? she wondered. Or excitement?

Not that she'd had much experience with fun times in

bed. After the initial honeymoon phase, sex during her marriage had been...disappointing.

With the vase of flowers tucked securely in the crook of her left arm, Poppy strolled across the parking lot toward her car. Though she'd left the bar alone, when she was a few feet from the vehicle a prickle along her skin told her she had company. She glanced toward her left in time to see a man dressed in black step from the shadows.

Poppy's heart slammed against her ribs. Tense muscles rippled. She lifted the vase, poised to fling the flowers in the mugger's direction and run.

But before she could get her arms to move, the light from a full moon played over the handsome face. Her fear deflated as quickly as a balloon pricked by a sharp pin.

"Ben." She lowered the vase, pressing her hands firmly against the crystal to still their trembling. "You startled me."

"Apologies." His cultured voice reminded her of expensive bourbon, the kind that slid down smooth but packed a wallop. "You were stunning tonight. Your voice is tailor-made for sexy, sultry songs."

On the surface, he'd offered a simple compliment. But the look in his eyes told her it wasn't just her voice he found sexy.

The truth was, she found him sexy, too. When she saw him sitting in the audience, dressed simply in black pants and a sweater, her heart had quaked. This was a man who looked good in everything...and probably even better in nothing at all.

Poppy's cheeks heated. She dropped her gaze toward the roses, now protected from the cool night air by a tent of cellophane. "Thank you for the compliment. And for the lovely flowers. They smell every bit as good as they look."

When Benedict didn't immediately respond, a horrible thought struck her. What if he wasn't the "Ben" who'd sent them?

Before she could backtrack, his lips stole upward in a

pleased smile. "The florist assured me you'd get them before the competition started. I'm happy to see he kept his word."

Break a leg, the note had said. Yes, Ben would have wanted her to receive them before she stepped onto the stage. Poppy saw no purpose in telling him the roses hadn't arrived until after her performance.

"I was cheering for you tonight," he added in a deep, sexy rumble. "Congratulations. You deserved the win."

Although Poppy had friends in the audience tonight, most—like Tripp—were there to support other contestants. The fact that Benedict had been there for *her* thrilled and terrified her.

"It was fun. Definitely a good cause." Poppy moved around him to open her car door, trying to ignore the alarming rush of sheer physical awareness at his nearness.

In a self-preservation move, she took an obscene amount of time placing the flowers—secured in the cardboard carrier the florist had left—on the passenger-side floorboard. Yet when she straightened, Benedict was still there.

Poppy raised the collar of her coat and shoved her hands into the pockets. Taking a steadying breath, she cocked her head. "What is it you want?"

Her question was blunt, to the point and totally unnecessary. The look in his eyes proclaimed in big neon letters exactly what he wanted, or rather *who* he wanted.

He wants me. She fought a surge of pleasure at the thought, a pleasure that sharply spiked when Ben pulled her to him.

"I'd like—" he paused and a slight smile lifted his lips "—to know if you have plans for the rest of the evening?"

He smelled like soap and an indefinable male scent that made her want to lean into him. Instead she made herself focus on the question.

Plans? Yes, she had plans. Of course she had plans. But what were they? And why, now basking in the heat from his body, did they suddenly seem so irrelevant?

"I—I do," Poppy finally managed to stammer.

His hands dropped and he moved from her, taking the warmth with him.

"I wasn't aware you were seeing anyone." An emotion she couldn't identify flickered in the molten silver of his eyes. "Who is he?"

"Rocky." Her grin came quick and fast, surprising them both. "Rocky Road."

Beneath the expensive cut of his dark wool coat, Ben's shoulders relaxed. The harsh planes of his face softened, making him look younger and more vulnerable. Approachable.

"You may not be aware—" He reached out and adjusted her collar. When his fingers brushed her neck, Poppy was disconcerted to feel her breath quicken. "—that Rocky and I are well acquainted."

"Yeah, well, Rocky gets around."

He chuckled, a low pleasant rumbling sound, his gaze lingering on her lips. "Have dinner with me. Rocky can wait."

"Ben." While he hadn't given her permission to use it, the name came easily. Poppy liked the way it felt on her tongue. Liked it a little too much, she realized.

Poppy started to rake her fingers through her hair then stopped when she realized she'd muss the waves Cassidy had labored so hard to perfect. God, she was confused.

The only certainty was that accepting a dinner invitation from this man would be a first step down a path she had no intention of traveling. Spontaneous was one thing. Foolhardy quite another. "I don't believe our having dinner is a good idea."

Poppy immediately realized her mistake when puzzlement filled his gray eyes. She should have simply lied and said she'd eaten before the show. Or been completely honest and confessed she was fighting an urge to feast on him.

"Why isn't it a good idea?" he asked, leveling a steady gaze.

While Poppy was telling herself to shut this down and get in her car, Ben shot her a wolfish grin showing a mouthful of perfect white teeth.

"I promise I won't bite." He lifted his right hand and offered a two-fingered salute. "Scout's honor."

The thought of this prominent physician ever sleeping in a tent or starting a fire with sticks brought a laugh to Poppy's lips. "You were never a scout."

"I made it all the way to Eagle."

"I was a Brownie."

This time it was his turn to laugh.

Poppy tilted her head. "Do you have badges?"

"A whole box of them," he said with a sheepish smile. "How about you?"

"I have a whole box, too," Poppy said rashly.

"Really?"

His tone was clearly skeptical and, well, it rankled. She was positive—or almost positive—that she had five or six badges packed away...somewhere. And six was *almost* a boxful.

Feeling suddenly relaxed, Poppy ignored the warning flags popping up in her head.

"I'll show you my badges if you show me yours," she taunted.

"You've got a deal." He caught her hand in his, lifted it to his mouth and pressed a kiss against her wrist before she could stop him.

She jerked her hand back, the warm moist imprint of his lips searing her skin.

He smirked. "If there's going to be a badge showing tonight, we'll need to fuel up. Dinner then badges. It's part of the deal."

Deal? For a second, panic clogged her throat. They didn't have a deal. She'd been merely enjoying a little lighthearted conversation. Okay, and maybe practicing her rusty flirting skills. Some very rusty skills. Even a high-school girl would know better than to bring up *scouting* badges.

Poppy cleared her throat, searching for a painless way out of this mess. "Even if I agreed to dinner, all the restaurants in Jackson Hole are booked for the evening."

"A challenge." His gray eyes reminded her of a shimmery fog. "Do you like Italian?"

Though the wind had picked up, Poppy wasn't cold. Heat, mixed with an intoxicating dose of testosterone, rolled off him and wrapped around her. "Doesn't everyone? But—"

"Hold that thought." He pulled a slim phone from his pocket, waited a few seconds for the call to connect then asked for Angelo. "Tell him it's Ben Campbell." A moment later, he confirmed a table for two.

He pocketed the phone. Satisfaction blanketed his face. "We have a reservation at the Trattoria."

Poppy's resolve to keep her distance wavered as her stomach emitted a low growl. Visions of her favorite pasta dish danced in her head. "The Ravioli di Granchio is my favorite."

Ben smiled. "What's not to love about large ravioli stuffed with stone crab and shrimp in a creamy lobster sauce?"

"I'm impressed."

"Don't be," he said with a laugh. "My familiarity with the menu merely tells you how often I eat out."

"How did you get a reservation? The place was booked solid for tonight." Poppy distinctly remembered Lexi mentioning that fact to her only last week.

He merely shrugged.

Poppy wondered who Angelo was and what his connection was to Ben. Before she could press for details he slanted a dismissive glance at her small Ford. "We'll take my vehicle. I'll bring you back after dinner to pick up yours."

She began shaking her head before he finished speaking.

Riding with him would make the evening feel more like, well, a date. She didn't want to date Ben Campbell. Sharing a meal with an acquaintance, a friend of a friend, was as spontaneous as she wanted to be this evening. Poppy planned to enjoy the ravioli before heading home to Rocky.

"I'll meet you at the restaurant." Instead of drill sergeant brisk, as Poppy had intended, her voice sounded oddly breathless. As if she'd spent the past five minutes running uphill instead of standing still.

His mouth tightened briefly. For a moment she thought he might argue. After a heartbeat, the determined look on his face eased. "Fine."

Poppy glanced down as if she could see the WWII era dress through her cashmere coat. "I should go home and change."

"Please don't." He placed a hand on her shoulder. "The dress is very pretty."

"But hardly...modern." She found it difficult to think when he stood so near she could see the faint hint of stubble on his jawline. "I wouldn't want to embarrass you."

His brows pulled together as if trying to make sense of the sarcasm in her tone.

"Will *you* be uncomfortable wearing it?" he asked after a long moment.

"No." Poppy liked the dress, liked the way it accentuated her curves. Liked the way it made her feel pretty and feminine.

He reached around to open the car door. "I'll see you at the restaurant."

Poppy shifted from one foot to the other. She furrowed her brow. Was she worrying for nothing? It was just dinner, right?

Apparently sensing the evening's plans still hadn't been solidified, Ben brushed his knuckles across the curve of her cheek. "Trust me." His voice was smooth, persuasive. "We'll have a good time."

As Poppy stared into those liquid silver eyes, she realized that's just what had her scared.

Chapter Four

By the time the waiter brought out the tiramisu, Poppy had to admit Ben kept his promise. From the moment they'd been escorted to a table in a cozy alcove that felt private despite the crowded restaurant, it had been a lovely evening.

The doctor appeared to be a regular at the Trattoria. Once they were seated, the waiter asked if he'd like a bottle of his favorite wine brought over. Angelo, who Poppy discovered was the owner, stopped by for a few minutes after they'd finished the main course to make sure everything was satisfactory.

Angelo raved about her "bel vestito" and when Ben enthusiastically agreed it was indeed a very pretty dress, Poppy felt the last of her embarrassed tension slip away. After explaining about the Torch Singing competition, he made Poppy produce the silver microphone trophy from her purse for Angelo to admire.

Ben's enthusiasm took her by surprise. Perhaps he wasn't *exactly* like her ex-husband, who would have been horrified by her participation in such an event. And he certainly never would have agreed to go out for dinner with her dressed in circa 1943 garb.

After refilling her glass of wine, Ben lifted his own into the air. "To new friendships."

Finding nothing objectionable about such a toast, Poppy tapped her glass against his. The crystal sang. When she lowered the glass, she realized he was staring.

She raised a hand to her cheek. "Do I have something on my face?"

He gave a slow sideways shake of his head before his lips lifted in a lazy smile.

She wondered if Ben was aware how irresistible he looked at that moment. "Then what?"

"You're incredibly lovely."

Embarrassed, yet oddly pleased, Poppy gave a shaky laugh. "Right back at you."

Ben chuckled and it took everything she had not to blather and insist it was the truth. His chiseled jaw held the merest hint of a shadow, which only added to his attractiveness quotient. And then there were those silver eyes...

Heat raced through her body to pool between her thighs. It had to be the wine, she decided. She set down the glass she'd lifted for the toast and told herself it was time to switch to coffee.

Ben watched her for a second longer then his gaze flicked to the right. The waiter, dressed in dark pants and a crisp white shirt, immediately moved tableside.

"We'll take coffee now," Ben informed him.

"Of course, sir." The man slipped silently away.

Poppy took a sip of water, disturbed by his take-charge behavior. "What makes you think I want coffee?"

"It goes well with dessert." Ben gestured to the tiramisu. Seconds later the waiter placed the coffee on the table.

Ignoring the steaming brew, Poppy glanced around the crowded room. Her gaze lingered on a couple holding hands.

They were staring into each other's eyes with such passion Poppy swore she saw a fat little cupid and pink hearts floating above them. She exhaled a sigh.

Ben lightly touched her arm. "Problem?"

She shifted her gaze back to him. Her mouth twisted in a wry smile. "Well, for starters it's Valentine's Day and I'm out with you."

The coffee cup paused several inches from his lips. "That's flattering."

"Oh, my goodness, that didn't come out right. I didn't mean—" She stopped prattling when she saw a faint look of amusement in his eyes. "It's just that we're…strangers."

"Isn't that why we're here?" At her blank look, he continued. "To get to know each other."

He reached over and covered Poppy's hand with his, his eyes mesmerizing.

"Tell me why you decided to become a social worker," he continued in a deep sexy rumble that made her insides quake.

She'd told him about her childhood in Jackson Hole over dinner. But when she'd reached her college years, the conversation had taken a turn to favorite books and movies.

Other than mentioning he'd been sent back East to boarding school at twelve, Ben had kept the conversation squarely focused on her. Poppy had gone along, convinced if she asked too many questions, it might give the erroneous impression she was interested in him.

Slipping her hand out from under his, she kept her answer short and sweet. "I started out in fashion merchandising. But I had to do some volunteer work to satisfy a humanities requirement and a free clinic was close to campus."

He leaned slightly forward, offered an encouraging smile.

"Since the sight of blood makes me queasy, I was assigned to help in the social services area." It had been an eye-opening experience for the young sorority girl. "Marlene, the social worker there, was inspiring. Helping people felt right. After that semester I changed my major and never looked back."

"I applaud you." Ben forked off a piece of tiramisu. "Servicing the public isn't always easy. People who need help often don't want it. And sometimes a person's worst enemy is themselves."

Though he'd kept his tone offhand, something in the words sparked Poppy's interest. *Don't ask. Don't ask.*

"Sounds to me like you've had some personal experience with such people," she heard herself say.

She thought he might refuse to share. Hoped he would. Then his eyes met hers and she saw the frustration.

Ben lifted one hand and began counting off fingers. "Not returning for follow-up appointments. Not doing the therapy they've been given. Letting the kid jump on the bed when they have a cast so the child ends up reinjuring themselves."

Poppy grimaced at the sudden image of a small boy tumbling to the floor and a healing bone resnapping like a brittle tree branch.

Bringing the dessert to his lips, Ben chewed, swallowed. "I don't understand it."

He cared, she grudgingly admitted, and obviously wanted the best for all his patients. Including patients who—for whatever reason—were noncompliant.

After several years in the social work field, Poppy often likened human behavior to a thousand-piece jigsaw puzzle. A stiff look at each individual piece was usually necessary before one could understand where the segment fit into the big picture.

"It could be a cultural or a language issue," she murmured. "Or something as simple as the postoperative instructions needing to be more basic. Often there's more than one reason we don't do what's best for us."

She was seconds away from offering to consult on these issues when she clamped her lips together. The fact she was tempted to prolong the conversation was a red flag.

"What you're saying makes sense." He lifted the bottle and refilled her wineglass before topping off his. "I realize there can be extenuating circumstances. It just gets frustrating to repair a fractured bone or a torn tendon and then not have it heal correctly because the patient doesn't do their part."

"I'm sure it does." Poppy took another sip of the dry but zesty white. "Tell me how you're currently dealing with those patients."

"Some other time perhaps." Ben waved a dismissive hand. "I didn't bring you here tonight to bore you with talk of my problem patients."

No, Poppy thought, remembering what he'd said only moments before. *He wants us to get better acquainted.* A shiver traveled up her spine.

Well, she certainly didn't want him to probe any further into *her* life. A few questions more about her work history and the only topic left would be the extremely personal tale of her ill-fated marriage. It was a time she didn't like to revisit even on the best of days. That meant she must keep the focus off of her. "Did you always want to be a doctor?"

His eyes lit up, apparently pleased by her interest. "With my grandfather and father both being physicians, medicine has been a part of my life for as long as I can remember."

Poppy absently took a sip of wine. "What made you decide to go with the same specialty as your dad?"

"It was a perfect fit." Ben's gaze grew thoughtful. "I enjoy doing what's necessary to make a person whole again."

"I think it'd be stressful." Poppy had done a stint in the hospital when she was in training. She remembered the orthopedic patients and their often lengthy surgeries.

"I work well under pressure," he said with a hint of a smile. "And I'm good with my hands."

Poppy couldn't stop herself. Her gaze dropped to his fingers that were currently wrapped around the wineglass. Strong, straight fingers with short filed nails. Large, talented hands that could finesse surgical tools or a woman's breast—

She inhaled sharply and glanced up. Her gaze locked with Benedict's and a volatile heat swirled around her. Around him.

Around them.

"I want you, Poppy." His low tone stirred her already overheated blood. The longing that had been aroused earlier by him simply touching her hand morphed into a full-fledged ache. "I have ever since we kissed at the party."

She tried to keep the intense feelings from showing but knew she hadn't been successful when satisfaction blanketed his face.

"You want me, too," he said quietly.

He was completely and totally right. But to say so would take them places she couldn't, wouldn't, go.

"No. No, I don't." Her voice sounded shaky and faint, as if it had traveled a long distance.

His gaze dropped pointedly to her chest where her breasts strained against the fabric, yearning for his touch.

From another part of the restaurant, a woman began to sing an aria from *Don Pasquale.* Poppy fought the urge to fall into hysterical laughter. The beautiful music, the golden glow of candlelight and the sweet scent of flowers spun a seductive web.

Still, she wasn't foolish enough to believe what she felt had anything to do with romance.

Lust, yes.

Romance, no.

Poppy consumed the last of the Jermann Vinnae in her glass. "I've never had a one-night stand. Never been tempted."

"I don't make a habit of that kind of thing, either." Ben's voice sounded as matter-of-fact as hers.

Thankfully he didn't hint that this needn't be a onetime thing, or intimate he'd be open to more. If he had that would have been enough to send her fleeing to her car and heading home.

The fact that there were no expectations meant she was free to consider the possibility of a night of simple pleasure. Poppy couldn't remember the last time sex had been fun, easy or spontaneous.

Could she really use this man for sex? Yet, would it really be using him if he wanted it, too?

"If we decide to extend the evening—" Poppy lifted her chin even as heat spiked up her neck "—we'd need to establish a few ground rules."

"Such as?"

It was a question easy enough to answer. Then why Poppy wondered, did she feel as if she were standing on an unstable shore, poised to plunge into water where she'd be over her head in seconds?

Take a step back, she told herself.

But when Ben took her hand and his thumb began to lightly caress her palm, Poppy's brain faltered. She knew there were several important points she should clarify, but right now she couldn't think of one.

"The most important rule is to make the night count," she heard him say.

"Night?" She shook her head to clear the fog. "It shouldn't take more than an hour." *And that's probably being generous.*

His lips twitched. "The heat between us is hot enough to melt iron. We need to give ourselves time."

Ben brought her fingers to his mouth in a leisurely gesture that made her stomach clench. Each separate tip sizzled beneath his lips.

Alarm bells rang. Poppy thought about pulling back but told herself if she was seriously considering having sex with Ben, this casual intimacy could be viewed as a logical first step in that process. Besides, it felt too good to ask him to stop.

After a moment, he lowered her hand and laced his fingers through hers. She inhaled sharply when his thumb began to stroke the top of her hand.

"Don't shortchange yourself," Ben told her.

He obviously meant the words to be encouraging, but instead they were a splash of cold water. Wouldn't shortchanging herself be exactly what she'd be doing if she followed through on this plan? No, that was her mother's voice whispering the warning in her ear. Hers was the one telling her to stop overthinking and go for spontaneous.

"I'm not the type to shortchange myself," she said firmly.

"Me, either." He grinned. "That's why we're well-suited."

She straightened abruptly and jerked her hand from his.

"In terms of going after what we want," he said in a calming tone, his expression bland. "Neither of us is interested in pretending that tonight is about anything more than quenching a good old-fashioned case of lust."

Relief flooded Poppy as the waiter appeared with the check. Before she could pull out her wallet, the server took Ben's credit card and disappeared.

"I'm paying for my own meal." Poppy tugged a couple of bills from her purse and shoved them across the table. "And half the wine."

"I invited you. This is a celebration." He pushed her money back toward her.

Poppy puffed out her cheeks then reluctantly nodded. "Thank you."

When the waiter returned and effusively wished them a fabulous evening, his enthusiasm told Poppy he'd gotten a huge tip. Ben hadn't disappointed him. Poppy hoped he wouldn't disappoint her either.

But first things first...

"Birth control," she said once the waiter walked away. It was simply a little necessary housekeeping. Being wild and crazy didn't mean being stupid.

Ben's brows rose. "I assume you're on the pill."

"Actually, I'm not," Poppy admitted and saw surprise flash in his eyes. "My husband and I weren't able to have children. No cause was ever determined but Bill had already fathered two children during his first marriage so it had to be me."

Poppy waited for the look of sympathy. When it thankfully didn't come, she continued. "Then I found out he'd been unfaithful—"

"He cheated on you?" The shock on Ben's face was too real to be faked.

"Almost from day one." Poppy's laugh lacked any humor. "I was too stupid to see it."

"You trusted him." Ben's expression softened. "He was the fool."

A lump formed in Poppy's throat, but she determinedly swallowed past it. "The point is, when I discovered his infidelity, I had every STD test known to man. I haven't been with anyone since."

When her gaze landed on Ben, he seemed to understand she needed a similar assurance. "I'm clean, too."

Poppy nodded. Though Ben had a reputation for being arrogant, he also was known as a straight shooter. If he said he was clean, she could accept his word.

"Still, we'll use condoms," he said, as if anticipating her next request.

She looked over his shoulder, to all the couples laughing and talking with the ones they loved. *Is this what my life has come to?*

Before Poppy let herself become maudlin, she reminded herself she'd already tried the traditional route. Where had *that* gotten her?

"No reason to take chances," he added when she didn't respond.

"But we are taking a chance." Poppy chewed on her lower lip. "Making lov—er having sex, is not the same as getting together with someone on the golf course. Heck, we could both be duds."

Poppy thought back to all those romantic evenings she'd planned that had ended up falling flat. Her heart twisted. No, she couldn't make any guarantees in that area.

Benedict shot her a wink. "I'm not worried."

Well, that made one of them.

Poppy grabbed her bag. "We might as well get started."

She'd show him that she could be as spontaneous and as good in bed as the next woman.

His smile widened at her businesslike tone. "Might as well."

"We can meet at your house. I'll need your address." This way if things went south, she could simply walk out the door, instead of having to kick him out of her place.

His eyes met hers and her body began to tremble.

"When it's done, we walk away and never speak of this night again." Dear God, had those words actually come from her mouth?

Ben's look never wavered. "If that's how you want it."

Poppy stared into his eyes and felt her heart flip-flop. Had she really just negotiated the terms of a one-night stand? Yeah, spontaneity was definitely her middle name. "I'm sure some would call the arrangement cold-blooded."

"I've never set much stock by what others say," Ben said in that easy, confident way of his. "And we both know what's simmering between us right now is anything but cold."

Whether it was the wine, the teasing glint in his eyes or simply the relief at having the details worked out, Poppy laughed and did what she'd wanted to do all evening.

Leaning forward, she skimmed a finger down his cheek then kissed him full on the mouth. A heat hot enough to melt Alaska speared through her.

"Not cold." Her lips curved in a satisfied smile as she pulled back. "Not cold at all."

Chapter Five

On this night for romance the only tunes flowing from the radio in Poppy's bright red Ford Fiesta were love songs. As Luther wailed about the power of the most basic of emotions, Poppy watched Ben's sleek black sedan reach the edge of Jackson and turn west.

After carefully looking both ways, she turned onto the highway behind him and thought not of love, but of sex. Hot, quick and steamy. A shiver of anticipation coursed up her spine as she followed his Mercedes down the dark ribbon of asphalt toward the quiet residential area just outside of Jackson.

Though she hadn't seen his home, she was prepared to be impressed. Willowbrook boasted three-acre lots, an amazing view of Grand Teton and a plethora of native birds and animals.

When Ben turned into a driveway and motion lights flicked on, Poppy slowed her own vehicle and gaped. The surrounding wilderness provided a perfect backdrop for the two-story home with its dramatic stone entry.

A large expanse of winter white flowed like a blanket to the street. Perfectly landscaped trees and bushes pushed through pristine snow. As stunning as it was now, Poppy could only imagine how beautiful the yard would be in a few months when the trees were green and flowers and bushes in full bloom.

One of the garage doors slid smoothly up and Ben eased his car into the opening. Almost immediately, a second rose.

Poppy hesitated only an instant before pulling inside. She supposed it made sense to have her vehicle under wraps. No sense advertising to the neighbors he was "entertaining." The door slid silently down as Poppy stepped from her car to the sound of staccato barks coming from inside the house.

Ben glanced over the top of her car, a question in his eyes. "I should have asked before now if you're allergic to dogs."

When she shook her head, relief crossed his face.

"Angela was leaving at five so he's been alone for several hours." As the barking continued, Ben glanced in the direction of the door. "Don't let that racket worry you. Groucho loves people."

Poppy heard fondness in his tone. She assumed Groucho was the dog. But the woman's identity—and her relationship to Ben—remained a mystery. "Who's Angela?"

"My housekeeper." He waited while Poppy rounded the front of her car. "She cooks, cleans and takes care of Groucho."

Does she also take care of you? Poppy wondered, then immediately reminded herself *that* information was none of her business. Still, she was curious.

"How long has she worked for you?" Her voice came out casual and offhand, just as she intended.

"Five years." They crossed a spotless garage floor to the door leading inside the house, his hand resting lightly against her back. "Her days and hours vary, depending on my schedule. I appreciate the fact she's flexible."

He keyed in a few numbers to unlock a security system then pushed open a door, stepping aside to let Poppy enter.

"Groucho, sit," Ben called from behind her, and the small silver-and-black schnauzer dropped midleap to sit at her feet.

The dog's entire body wiggled as if filled with a bag of jumping beans. His beautiful dark eyes shifted from Benedict to Poppy. A whine hummed from the back of his throat.

Benedict squatted down and picked up the dog, giving him an affectionate hug, scrubbing his hand across the top of the furry head. "How's my boy?"

Groucho responded by licking his neck, bringing a laugh to Benedict's lips. "Yeah, I'm happy to see you, too."

He turned the animal in his arms, tucking him securely against his body. "Poppy, this is Groucho. He's only two, so he still has lots of puppy in him."

Poppy tentatively stroked the dog's fur and received her own appreciative lick on the hand. "He's a handsome boy."

"I think so." Grabbing a leash from a rack, Benedict clipped it to the dog's red collar and placed him on the floor. He shot Poppy an apologetic look. "I should take him outside for a few minutes."

"I'll come with you." While she stood on the sidewalk alongside the garage, Ben let Groucho check out various trees and bushes. "It surprises me you have a dog."

He looked mildly amused. "Why is that?"

"For starters, you're a busy man."

"There's more to life than practicing medicine." Ben gestured toward the animal inspecting a small bush shaped like a globe. "He was found abandoned out on Route 22, near Brown's curve, when he was six months old. His leg and a couple ribs were fractured."

Poppy's breath caught. She brought a hand to her chest. "He'd been hit by a car?"

"He'd been hit." Benedict's lips thinned. "But not by a vehicle."

"Someone hurt then dumped him?" Anger warred with the shock in her voice.

"That's how it appeared." For a second Ben's eyes flashed then he lifted a shoulder. "Anyway, a friend at the animal shelter told me about him. He needed a home. I had one."

The dog appeared content and happy as he wandered from bush to bush. It was difficult to imagine he'd had such a rough beginning. As if aware of her sympathy, Groucho looked over his shoulder at her and wagged his tail.

"I bet he misses you during the day."

"Sometimes." Ben chuckled. "Other times I don't think he notices…or cares. Especially on the days Angela brings her granddaughter with her. He's crazy about kids."

Poppy wasn't sure what surprised her most. That the woman she'd envisioned as a dark-haired temptress was a grandmother or that the doctor could be so accommodating. "You don't mind her bringing a child with her while she's working?"

"Why should I?" Puzzlement filled his gray eyes. "Liliana is well-behaved. And, as I said, Angela is flexible so I try to be, too."

Though Ben acted as if the concession was no big deal, Poppy knew it would have been a different story at her New York penthouse. Her ex obviously hadn't minded stealing their housekeeper away from her duties for sex, but he'd have been horrified if she'd ever had the temerity to ask to bring her child with her to work.

"Looks like he's ready to head inside," Ben announced.

Instead of reentering the home through the garage, Ben steered her toward the front door. While he put away the leash and wiped Groucho's feet in the entryway, Poppy's curiosity propelled her farther into the house.

With its amber-colored walls, massive stone fireplace

and intricately woven rugs on shiny hardwood, the large room with the soaring ceilings had a surprisingly cozy feel.

Feet now clean and dry, the dog padded across the room to hop onto a leather sofa. After rearranging a navy blanket into a makeshift nest, he settled down to gnaw contently on a small green bone.

Ben hung up their coats before he returned to her side. "Can I interest you in a tour?"

The gleam shimmering in his eyes told her exactly what room he'd like to show her.

Poppy shivered.

"Cold?" He captured her hand and brought her fingers to his lips. "Let's see if I can warm you up."

With brilliant gray eyes focused on hers, he kissed each finger lightly then pressed a kiss into her palm.

A sizzle of electricity shot up her arm. Heat flooded her body.

Ah, yes. This was the reason she was here—with him— this evening.

"I'd love to see your—" she paused and offered him what she hoped was an enigmatic smile "—the rest of your lovely home."

Ben took her hand. "Come with me."

With his fingers laced loosely through hers, he took her through a state-of-the-art kitchen with commercial grade appliances and enough cabinet space to make her drool. She was still thinking that those cupboards could hold anything an aspiring gourmet cook could ever want when Ben ushered her down the hall to show her several bedrooms, bathrooms and his home office. Then they headed up the curving stairs to the second level.

The suite that encompassed most of the upper floor was clearly designed for comfort. Especially if one equated comfort with space. There was a bed the size of Wyoming and a sitting area large enough to hold a couple of neighboring states, as well.

Conscious of Benedict's perusal, Poppy strolled past a desk with triple screen monitors to peer into a closet with enough clothes and shoes to fill a small department store. But in her mind, next to the magnificent bed, the pièce de résistance was the bathroom.

With a wealth of natural lighting, sleek stone floor and a shower with knobs and spray heads reminding her of a car wash, the luxury—and the decadence of it all—stole her breath.

"That—" Poppy gestured toward the glass-enclosed shower big enough for a party of five "—is a fantasyland. If I got in there to play, you'd never get me out."

His gaze slid slowly over her and she got the distinct feeling he was imagining her inside those glass walls...naked.

Her skin prickled. She wondered if he suspected she'd been envisioning him in there with her, also sans clothes.

Turning back to the sitting area with its arched window and massive stone fireplace, Poppy stepped toward the warmth and held out her hands.

Out of the corner of her eye, she saw Groucho bound into the room and make a beeline for a dog pillow next to the desk, a tiny green bone sticking out of his mouth.

Ben gestured toward a long sofa in muted peach. "Would you like some wine?"

Though a nice glass of red sounded good, more alcohol was the last thing Poppy needed. If she was going to have sex, she'd at least like to remember it. With more than a little regret, she shook her head.

Ben moved close, his hand cupping the back of her neck. "You're right. We have something more pressing on the agenda."

His mouth closed over hers with a hunger that made her heart stutter. Still, he didn't rush. As if they had all the time in the world, he continued to kiss her, slow, leisurely kisses that stoked the fire in her belly.

"You're so beautiful," he murmured, his lips against her hair, his arms strong around her.

Breathing in the spicy scent of him, Poppy reveled in the warmth of his embrace. She raked her fingers through his thick dark strands and found them soft as silk. "You're kind of pretty yourself."

The corner of his mouth twitched. He laughed softly, a deep rumbling sound that pleased her.

"I'm not exactly sure what I'm doing," she whispered, then paused, not sure what else to say.

"Tonight we'll be lovers." With one finger he gently brushed back a lock of her hair that had tumbled from its glittery clip.

"Yes," she answered, her voice as unsteady as her heartbeat. "Yes, we will."

"It's been a while for you." He spoke softly.

"After my divorce I swore off men." Poppy stepped from his arms and took a seat on the sofa, smoothing her skirt with a sweaty palm.

"What made you change your mind?" Ben took a seat next to her.

"You."

Time seemed to stretch and extend.

"That's flattering."

"For whatever reason, you brought those long-buried desires back to the surface." Though heat rose up her neck, Poppy refused to be embarrassed. "I hope I made it clear I'm not looking for a relationship."

He opened his mouth then closed it without speaking.

"For me that's a big part of the draw," she added.

His brows pulled together. "Draw?"

"I overthink everything. But not tonight. I'm going with the moment, being spontaneous." Poppy took a deep breath then let it out slowly.

When he only continued to stare, she felt compelled to fill the void.

"It's been a long time since sex was fun," she murmured almost defensively.

The moment her eyes touched his, something inside her seemed to lock into place and she couldn't look away. Sensation licked up her arm, down to her breasts to pool between her thighs. Abruptly Poppy stood, kicked off her shoes and began to unbutton her dress. "Let's do it."

He laughed again, this time a full-bodied laugh that relaxed the lines in his face. Pulling himself to his feet, his fingers closed over her hand. "What's the rush? We have all night."

She stilled. "I never agreed to stay over."

His hesitation was so brief, it was barely noticeable. "It's a figure of speech."

"Oh."

"I simply meant there is no reason we can't take our time." He gestured toward the hearth. "Enjoy the fire. Enjoy each other."

Poppy understood. While she found nothing objectionable with the sentiment, she worried taking so much time would make the act more intimate. More like lovemaking. Less like a fun, no-strings romp. "I'd rather get down to business."

Those silvery eyes studied her for several heartbeats before his lips curved and he tugged her to him.

His mouth closed over hers, hot and searing. The taste of him pushed any lingering misgivings far, far away. Doubts had no place here. Not tonight. If she ended up with regrets, she'd deal with them tomorrow. For now she would savor and enjoy.

Poppy couldn't quite remember ever being kissed like this, deep hungry kisses that shot fire to her belly. His hands were everywhere, unfastening buttons and zippers, his mouth voracious on hers. When Poppy came up for air, they were on the bed and naked.

Apparently he wasn't *really* interested in taking things

slow. Her lips curved as she ran her hand down his chest toward the evidence of his desire.

He clamped his hand around her wrist.

"Not so fast," he warned, with a half laugh. "Or this will be over before it has barely begun."

Inclining her head, Poppy batted her lashes. "Don't tell me you have only one condom?"

He grinned. "Darlin', I have a whole boxful."

Relief mixed with alarm. A *boxful?*

With a laugh, he rolled on top of her and fastened his mouth to hers. His fingers teased her nipples to hardened buds before his mouth lowered to replace his hand. The warmth in her lower belly turned fiery hot and became a pulsating need.

She squirmed, pressing her hips upward, wanting more of him. When his hand slipped between them to cup her and one finger slid inside, she moaned. "Please."

Though his breath grew ragged, he didn't rush. His mouth caressed her neck, trailing love bites upward as his hands stroked and kneaded and caressed.

Raw pleasure rippled through her and her body surged like an engine approaching overload. Never had she felt so alive, so in the moment. The carnal desire she'd once thought gone forever had returned, hot and intense.

Poppy couldn't keep her hands and mouth off him. His skin was warm and salty beneath her tongue, his body taut and responsive as she boldly stroked and caressed. Communication was quickly reduced to moans and sighs and gasps.

She wanted him inside her, needed him inside her. Just as she was beginning to believe she couldn't go one second longer, he snagged a condom from the bedside table. As if understanding it had been a long time for her, he gently eased in while continuing to caress, to kiss, to suckle. Once she'd accepted him fully, he began to move with slow, steady strokes that brought bursts of delicious sensations to her body and a prayer to her lips.

"Please don't stop," she begged.

He took her mouth in a rough kiss. "Furthest thing from my mind."

Poppy chuckled then gasped, when he plunged deeper. A fresh wave of pleasure stole her breath. She clung to him, her nails scoring his back as once again the moment blurred in a dizzying array of want and need. Yet when she poised on the edge of exploding, she held back, the emotion so intense, so real, it somehow seemed wrong to be experiencing it here, with this...stranger.

"Let go," he urged, his eyes dark with desire.

"I can't."

"You can." He captured her mouth in a ravenous kiss and rocked his hips. "You will."

A cry tore from her lips as her control snapped and she tumbled over the edge. Seconds later he shuddered and called her name, then collapsed on top of her.

Poppy closed her eyes, overcome by a world that still swirled around her in a blur of sight and sound. She was still breathing hard when he rolled off her. But instead of getting up, he pulled her to him, kissing her neck, her face, her lips.

"Amazing." Even to her own ears, her voice sounded as if it came from a million miles away.

"A good word." His voice rasped, deep and unsteady. "Though hardly adequate."

"You know what I'd like." Her arms remained wrapped around his warm flesh, the solid muscles taut beneath her fingers.

"Another amazing experience?"

Her lips curved. "A shower."

He trailed a finger down her body. "May I join you?"

She lifted one shoulder slightly, keeping her eyes fixed on him. "It's your shower."

"It's your fantasy." As heat flooded her cheeks, he chuckled. "And it happens to be mine, as well."

He rolled over and swore.

She widened her eyes. "Problem?"

"I got bit in the butt." He pulled one of her glittery clips out from under him. "By this."

"Poor Ben." She chuckled. "Want me to kiss and make it all better?"

His eyes sparked. "I'll remind you of that when we're in the shower."

Once under the steaming jets, he didn't need to remind her. Her desire was insatiable and he shared the obsession. There was only one bad moment.

He'd taken her against the glass block wall of the shower with streams of water washing over them, but when he pulled out, the condom slipped.

For a second he froze, as still as any museum statue. "We might have a problem."

Recalling all those years of monitoring her temperature, of having sex on precisely the right day and still not conceiving, Poppy simply laughed and kissed him. "No worries. Remember, I can't get pregnant."

Ben released a long breath. "I've never had this happen."

"It must be a night for firsts." Poppy trailed her hand slowly up and down his slick body.

He angled his head.

"I've never had sex three times in one night."

"We've only done it twice."

"That's true." She gave him a saucy wink. "But the night is still young."

Chapter Six

Though he hadn't fallen asleep until after two, Ben's internal alarm woke him shortly before five. He opened his eyes and turned at the feeling of pressure against his arm.

He smiled when he saw Poppy sprawled facedown with one of her arms flopped over his. A sheet draped low across her hips. Gently he tugged out from under her. He let his eyes linger on the soft expanse of skin and felt his body stir.

When they'd made love that third time it had been just as spectacular as the other two. The condom slippage on the second round still troubled him, but Poppy didn't appear worried. Since she hadn't conceived during her failed marriage, it was doubtful one slip would do it.

A soft tapping of nails sounded against the hardwood floors. Ben turned and saw Groucho staring up at him, a low whine humming in his throat.

He brought a finger to his lips and shot the dog a warning glance. Just because he and Groucho were early risers didn't mean Poppy had to get up. Slowly, regretfully, Ben slid off the side of the bed, shivering as cool air hit his bare skin.

Before hitting the shower, he tugged the comforter up to Poppy's shoulders. She murmured something but continued to sleep, her dark hair tousled against the pillow.

The urge to make love to her again seized him, gripped him like a hand to the throat. He desperately wanted to bring a smile to her mouth and a laugh back to her lips while her heart hammered and her lush body quivered beneath him.

But Groucho whined again and necessity trumped desire.

After a quick shower—extra cold—Ben donned jeans and a black sweater before heading downstairs.

Normally Angela had coffee ready and Groucho fed before he hopped out of bed, but today was Sunday and her day off. So after a quick trip outside with the schnauzer, he brought out the kibble. While the dog chowed down, Ben ground beans and got the coffee started. Chores completed, he poured himself a tall glass of orange juice and contemplated the past twelve hours.

His desire for Poppy only burned hotter after their time in bed. He wanted to spend more time with her. Several times last night he almost suggested they forget this one-night stand nonsense, but had held back.

She'd made it very clear all she wanted from him was light, fun sex. Well, last night *had* been fun. And there'd been lots of sex.

The coffeemaker beeped and he poured himself a cup, remembering her responsiveness, her fearlessness in letting him know exactly what she liked. He smiled smugly. Now, thanks to him, she had some new favorites.

He wrapped his hands around the steaming mug. If Poppy was willing, he was definitely up for a repeat performance.

"Good morning."

The low, throaty tone immediately conjured up images of sweat-soaked sheets and tangled limbs. Poppy stood in the doorway, looking tousled but gorgeous in the same floral dress she'd worn last night.

"I came in search of coffee." Though her gaze never wavered, her tentative smile told him she wasn't as confident as she appeared.

"You've come to the right place." Grabbing the extra mug he'd placed on the counter, Ben filled it with a rich Columbian breakfast blend. "How do you like it?"

"Black and strong."

Groucho looked up from his now empty dish and trotted over to her, his tail wagging a welcome.

Keeping her eyes on Ben, she bent and gave the top of the dog's head an affectionate pat. "Good morning, Groucho."

When she straightened, Ben handed her a mug. He expected her to sit and savor. Instead she rested one arm on the counter and remained standing. She peered at him through lowered lashes.

"I need some direction from you, doctor." While she spoke she absently trailed a finger around the lip of the cup.

Ben's mouth went dry, remembering how she'd trailed that same finger down the length of him.

"I'm at your service," he managed to croak out.

"I'm not sure of proper protocol." She gestured with her hand in the direction of the front of the house. "Should I have slipped silently out the door? Left a note on the pillow, thanking you for a night of great sex? Or…?"

"Running off is always poor manners." Ben placed his cup on the counter then pulled out a frying pan. After setting it on the burner, he moved to the refrigerator for the bacon and eggs. "Proper protocol mandates you drink your coffee while I make us breakfast."

When she hesitated, he shot her a wink. "Doctor's orders."

Poppy rolled her emerald eyes. But when she settled into the chair and made an appreciative sound at the taste of the coffee, Ben let himself relax.

With well-practiced ease, he added butter to the pan, cracked the eggs then shifted his attention to the bacon. But his mind remained focused on the brunette in his kitchen.

Though one-night stands by their nature came with a built-in ending, in Ben's mind, last night had been a beginning. He wasn't ready to let Poppy simply walk out of his life.

Though he knew she'd vehemently deny it, there was a link between them. He wasn't sure where that connection came from or where it might lead, but he was open to exploring possibilities.

Poppy took another long sip of coffee then cocked her head. "Do you always make a big breakfast for your... guests?"

There was no way Ben was getting into a discussion of the previous women in his life. Adroitly, he sidestepped the question. "Big breakfasts are for weekends."

"Then you don't eat like this—" she gestured with one hand toward the plates he was heaping with food "—every day?"

"Hardly." Ben chuckled. "During the week, I usually have a protein shake chased by a cup of very strong coffee."

Poppy tried to keep a poker face even as a chill traveled up her spine.

In her experience, most successful surgeons were self-disciplined to a fault. Very focused on getting what they wanted. *Used* to getting what they wanted with little regard for anyone, or anything, else. That was why it was imperative she keep Ben at arm's length.

Too late, Poppy thought, laughter bubbling up. She'd hardly kept Ben at arm's length last night.

"Something funny?" He placed the plate of eggs, bacon and toast in front of her before taking a seat.

"I was thinking of last night."

His fork stopped short of his mouth. "Last night was humorous?"

"No," she said quickly, but couldn't stop the smile forming on her lips. "Well, other than that thing you did with—"

"Favorite of mine, too." His unexpected grin made her heart thump.

Then he lowered his head and kissed her softly on the mouth. It only took one taste for her to forget the need for restraint. She wrapped her arms around his neck and gave into the sensations sweeping through her body like an out-of-control wildfire. He was the one who finally drew back with a shaky laugh.

As they ate, Poppy kept the conversation deliberately light. Yet, even as they chatted easily, something hovered in the air between them, something she didn't want to examine too closely. Last night had exceeded her expectations. Unfortunately, instead of satisfying her, she yearned for more.

The idea of a repeat performance, as enticing as it was, sent little red flags popping up.

Poppy wished she could convince herself that as long as they kept whatever this was between them just about sex, it wouldn't hurt to see Ben again. But the intense heat that even a simple kiss could spark warned their relationship might not stay light and fun for long. There was a reason a one-night stand lasted only one night.

"That was an excellent breakfast," she said when he rose to clear the dishes. "Following a most excellent, er, superb night."

She stood, bent to give Groucho one quick scratch behind the ears before straightening. "I need to run. I'm sure our paths will cross again. Jackson Hole isn't that big."

Poppy started to extend her hand, then realized the gesture might be more insulting than polite. She let her hand drop to her side.

Ben's gaze met hers. "I thought we might spend the day together."

The fact that her heart leaped at the offer told her she was right to step back. "Not part of the rules."

Puzzlement filled his eyes. "Rules?"

"One night." She forced a bright smile. "You go your way. I go mine."

"I remember," he said easily. "But rules can always be altered with the consent of both parties."

Poppy gathered up her purse. "That's the sticking point, then."

"I don't see why." His voice dropped to that sexy rumble that sent a thrill up her spine. "As I said, I want to spend the day with you."

Holding on to her resolve with both hands, Poppy met his gaze. "And I want to stick to the rules."

The women's bathroom at the courthouse afforded little privacy, but now that the worry was in her head, Poppy couldn't wait a second longer. She decided the stall was private enough to take the pregnancy test she'd picked up that morning "just to ease her mind."

Her period, which for the past twenty years had arrived with military precision, had yet to make an appearance. Initially she blamed the delay on the stress of a new job. Until Ben had left another message asking her to call him. Apparently he wanted to confirm there had been no consequences to the condom slipping when they were together.

She'd just missed her second period. Poppy pulled the box from her purse and glanced at the directions. The step wasn't really necessary. She'd taken this same test more times than she could count during the years she'd been seriously trying to get pregnant. If anyone knew these specific directions, it was her.

She made quick work of the process. When she gazed down at the stick, her heart gave a little leap. She'd never seen a positive. Plenty of negatives. But never a...

Poppy blinked. Positive. Blinked again.

The thickness filling her chest made breathing difficult. She glanced down as if she could see through her navy skirt.

Was there really a baby growing inside her? How was that even possible?

Tears leaked. She brushed them back, took several deep breaths. Though this particular test was touted as being ninety-nine point nine percent reliable, she needed an expert opinion before she gave in to emotion. Thankfully, she had an appointment later today with Travis Fisher, her ob-gyn, to discuss "menstrual irregularities."

After all, no test was foolproof. But the stomach upset she'd been experiencing in the morning for the past few weeks and the breast tenderness told her that when she went in for her appointment, she needed to be prepared.

Prepared to be told she was finally pregnant.

"The blood test and the exam confirm what you suspected."

Poppy sat in a chair in Travis's office, her nails digging into the arms of the leather chair. "The doctor in New York said I was infertile."

Despite her outward calm, her insides trembled.

"We all make mistakes." Travis smiled then his expression quickly sobered. "There's nothing in the records you had transferred that shows you're anything other than a healthy young woman. No medical reason is documented that would indicate you're physically unable to conceive."

"Nothing except four years of trying to have a baby without any results." Poppy tried to keep the frustration from her voice as she recalled the years of monitoring her temperature and having regimented sex.

Travis stroked his chin. "Have you considered the problem may not have been yours?"

"My ex had two children from a previous marriage and a high-normal sperm count." Poppy took in some air and blew it out. "But that doesn't matter now. According to you, I'm pregnant."

"You are indeed." Travis's gaze searched hers. "How does that make you feel?"

"Stupid," she admitted, then grudgingly added, "and excited. That probably sounds crazy considering I'm on my own here, but I never thought I'd be able to have a baby."

"Conflicting emotions are to be expected."

Poppy gave a little laugh. "It must be my upbringing but I keep waiting for you to do the shocked voice and ask me what was I thinking?"

"That's for your mother." Travis shifted in his chair. "Besides, I'd be the last person to lay that on you."

She cast him a curious glance.

"Several years ago Mary Karen and I found ourselves in the same situation you're in right now."

"She was pregnant when you married?"

He nodded. "With twins. I'd always thought I didn't want children."

She thought of his patience with the five rambunctious kids under his roof. Of the love in his eyes when his gaze settled on his children, his wife. "You're so good with them."

"Marrying Mary Karen and becoming a dad were the best things that ever happened to me." He looked Poppy square in the eye. "What about your baby's father? Where does he fit in this picture?"

Poppy shifted in her seat. "He doesn't know."

"Is he aware pregnancy is a possibility?" The kindness in Travis's voice brought back the threatening tears.

Poppy started to shake her head then stopped, remembering Ben's phone message. "We haven't been together since…in a while."

He stared at her for a long moment. She wondered if Travis suspected it was Ben they were discussing.

"Do you know what you're going to do?" He spoke casually, as if they were simply talking over a glass of wine or cup of coffee.

"Do about what?"

"About the baby." Travis's eyes never left her face. "You have options."

The underlying question didn't initially register. When it did, her hand moved protectively to her flat belly. "I don't want an abortion if that's what you're asking."

Hot fury filled her voice.

"That's one option," Travis said easily. "But I was speaking more of adoption. There are lots of couples looking for a baby to love."

Maybe so, Poppy thought, but in her heart she knew that no one could love this child more than she would. "That's not an option, either. I want this child."

"You'll be a excellent mother." Travis gave her shoulder a gentle squeeze. He went on to explain what she could expect in the upcoming months, both in terms of office visits and in bodily changes. As if he understood how hard she pushed herself, he emphasized the importance of proper rest.

"This is so surreal." Emotion welled up and this time she couldn't stop the tears. She brushed them back, smiling a bit soggily when Travis handed her a tissue.

"I'm going to have a baby." Poppy heard the wonder in her voice. "And I'm happy about it, Travis. Given the circumstances that might seem strange to some people…"

Poppy's voice trailed off as she thought of her parents.

In her family love came first, then marriage, then babies. But they'd adjust and they'd be supportive. Ben's reaction was the unknown.

Pushing to her feet, Poppy stood, her heart pounding so hard she felt light-headed.

"A new life is a cause for celebration." Travis rose and extended his hand, clasping hers warmly. "Let me be the first to offer you congratulations."

Poppy blinked back tears and smiled. "Thank you, Travis."

Her phone rang as she left the clinic. When she saw the name on the readout, Poppy realized it was time to take Benedict Campbell's call.

Chapter Seven

Ben cranked the volume up on his car stereo, enjoying the pulsating beat. The sun was shining, the day unusually warm for April and he would be seeing Poppy soon.

He'd planned to go alone to the housewarming at Mitzi's new condo, but at the last minute had reached out to Poppy one more time. Not only had she accepted his invitation, she'd told him she was *happy* he'd called.

The relief that had surged at that word had made Ben realize how much he wanted to see her again. Not since Kristin—his one serious relationship back in residency— had Ben been this excited about a woman.

Pulling into a small parking lot next to an equally small two-story apartment building, Ben was surprised that the doors of the eight units opened to the elements, rather than to an inside hall. Not an ideal situation when one lived in a wintery climate.

Ben headed up the exterior stairs, noting that the weathered wood could benefit from a liberal dose of stain and sealer. At unit number five, a wooden cutout of a sunflower graced the door while a prickly brown mat offered a faded welcome.

After taking a steadying breath, Ben rapped his knuckles against the blue door. He wasn't sure what had made Poppy change her mind, but this time there would be no silly rules about not seeing each other again.

Looking as pretty as ever, Poppy opened the door with a cheery smile. Shiny dark hair brushed her shoulders and the glossy lip color made her pouty mouth resemble a plump strawberry. Trendy red glasses perched on her nose.

"Ben, it's nice to see you again." Poppy, her voice as sultry as her perfume, moved aside to let him enter. "Give me a second to grab a coat."

Stepping past her, Ben resisted the urge to brush a kiss on those cherry red lips. But he warned himself to take things slow. There would be lots of opportunities for kissing.

As Poppy reached into the closet, he couldn't help admiring the way the green sweater dress hugged her shapely curves. When she turned back, coat in hand, light danced off the bright multicolored stones resting against her chest.

She made an enticing—and difficult to resist—picture.

Ben pulled his attention up from her breasts, er, necklace. He forced his gaze past tempting lips and didn't stop until he'd reached her eyes.

"You look stunning." He tapped a finger against the red frames. "I like these."

To his surprise, Poppy flushed, nervously brushing hair back from her face. "I scratched my cornea and the doctor said no contacts for a few days. I hate to go out looking like this."

Confused, he pulled his brows together. "You wore them at the Fisher party."

Ben had fond memories of that night. At the retro party, Poppy's beehive hairstyle, exaggerated makeup and sixties-era attire had caught his eye. The sexy glasses had only added to her appeal.

Poppy cocked her head and thought for a second. "I only wore them that night because they went well with my costume."

"We had our first kiss under the mistletoe at that party," he reminded her.

"You do have a good memory." Poppy gave a little laugh and changed the subject. "Who's going to be at this house-warming?"

He helped her on with the jacket. "Knowing Mitzi, probably anyone she ever met."

"She was dating some football player." Poppy slipped an arm into the coat sleeve. "Will he be there?"

Ben was glad Poppy seemed well-informed. It saved him from having to explain again that he and Mitzi were simply friends and colleagues.

"Last I heard." Ben kept his tone offhand. "He's back in town, anyway."

On their way down the steep steps outside, he took Poppy's elbow to steady her. As they drove to his colleague's new digs in Teton Village, Poppy asked about his family. Ben dutifully relayed how his parents had enjoyed their recent trip to Italy.

"My mother is eager to go back." Ben lifted one shoulder. "But my father is still practicing medicine half-time and his schedule is pretty full."

Though Poppy had seen his parents' pictures often enough in society photos, she hadn't personally met them or any other members of Ben's family. She didn't even know if he had other relatives in the area. The uncertainty made her realize how little she knew about her baby's father. "Do you have siblings?"

"Two brothers. Adam is a cardiologist in Denver. David is a researcher in Omaha." He tightened his fingers on the steering wheel. "One sister, Josie."

A pain sliced his heart at the thought of his younger sister. It had been well over a year since anyone in the family had heard from her.

"Are they married? Have any kids?"

He jerked his thoughts back from the past.

"Both my brothers are married. Adam and Jane have two little girls, Grace and Hannah. David and Lori haven't even celebrated their first anniversary so it's a little soon for babies." He paused for a barely perceptible second. "Josie is still single."

For a second Ben thought, feared, Poppy would ask where Josie lived, what she was doing now. Questions he couldn't answer. Instead, she picked at a piece of lint on her coat.

"I bet you're getting lots of pressure."

"Pressure?"

"To settle down. Marry." She gave a little laugh. "Repopulate the earth."

He grinned. "I think the earth is doing just fine without me adding to the influx."

The words had barely left his lips when Ben remembered part of the reason for his follow-up calls. He'd needed to be certain there'd been no unintended consequences from the condom fiasco. But Poppy's expression was serene, her responding smile easy. He decided not to spoil the mood.

Pulling the Mercedes to a stop at an intersection, Ben impulsively took her hand, brought it to his mouth and lightly kissed her knuckles. "For tonight, making sure you enjoy yourself is my priority."

"Oh." Poppy breathed out the word.

Though they drove the rest of the way with the conversation impersonally centered on weather and local politics, the air in the car remained charged with electricity.

The building where Mitzi's condo was located blended modern with rustic and the location offered excellent access to the ski lifts. Because of Poppy's heels, Ben insisted they take the elevator to the third level. It was easy to pinpoint the exact location of the party by the conversational din spilling into the hall.

The door to Mitzi's unit was ajar. Ben simply pushed it open and ushered her inside. When he'd called this morning, Poppy had impulsively decided to smooth things over with him before dropping the bomb that she had a baby on board.

In her mind, it was a sensible approach to a situation neither of them had anticipated. As she glanced around the condo teeming with conversation and laughter, Poppy wished she knew Ben better, wished she could predict how he'd respond. Would he be angry? Deny the child was his?

The thought came out of left field and a pain as sharp as a knife sliced her heart. Until this moment, Poppy hadn't considered he might doubt he was the father.

"Poppy." Mitzi, football player boyfriend in tow, slipped through the crowd to wrap arms around Poppy and give her a quick hug. "I'm happy you made it."

Dressed in a gold wraparound dress with hair the color of walnut, the beautiful young surgeon could have stepped from the pages of a fashion magazine.

Tonight's stylish image was in sharp contrast to some of the bohemian and urban chic looks Ben's colleague often favored. Beside her, a tall broad-shouldered man with a warrior's stance and a short crop of blond hair gave Poppy a bold stare.

Mitzi made quick work of the introductions. Though their hostess seemed oblivious, Ben's eyes sharpened when Kelvin held Poppy's hand for several seconds longer than necessary. A moment later, Ben took Poppy's arm and told Mitzi—and Kelvin—they were going to mingle.

But Kelvin wasn't so easily put aside. Poppy caught his speculative gaze on her several times over the course of the evening. The football player made his move as she stood at the bar for a club soda while Ben picked up appetizers from the buffet table.

"Hey, beautiful." Kelvin flashed a brilliant smile before

launching into a series of compliments he'd obviously used before with much success.

Poppy listened to the well-honed conversational patter and tried not to scowl. Finally, he got to the point and asked for her phone number.

"Not interested," she said in a matter-of-fact tone that sent his eyebrows shooting skyward. His disbelieving expression said it all. Not want him? How was that even possible?

It took Poppy almost a full minute to convince him she wasn't kidding, wasn't giving her his number and wasn't ever going out with him.

"Your loss" and a shrug were Kelvin's only responses.

He'd barely swaggered off in the direction of a perky blonde when Ben returned with the appetizers.

Poppy snagged a carrot stick and took a bite.

"Looks like Kelvin has you in his crosshairs," Ben said in a deceptively casual tone.

"Even if I didn't have a firm rule against poaching, Mr. Slick is the last man I'd ever want." Poppy made a face. "Mitzi should run far away from that one."

"Agreed." Ben's gray eyes were now the color of steel. "Yet, I can see why you caught his eye."

Poppy simply rolled her eyes and popped another piece of carrot into her mouth.

"You're not only sexy, you're incredibly intelligent." Unexpectedly Ben grinned. "As evidenced by your disinterest in him. And your interest in me."

His wink lightened the immodest statement.

Poppy chuckled, then realized she was having way too much fun. Perhaps she should have met Ben for coffee and simply given him the news straight out.

"How's the job going?" he asked when she remained silent.

"I like it." Poppy thought of the little girl she'd removed

from an abusive home earlier that afternoon. "Though it can be intense. It doesn't help I've been so tired lately—"

She stopped, warned herself not to go there. Not yet.

Ben's brows furrowed. "You're not sleeping well?"

"Too much partying, I guess," she said in a flippant tone. Which was a joke considering she hadn't been out socially since Valentine's Day.

His eyes cooled.

"Sheesh." Poppy rolled her eyes. "I was joking about the partying, Ben. Most nights I'm in bed by eight. Alone."

She wondered why she'd felt compelled to explain. Still, when the tense set of his jaw eased, Poppy was able to breathe again.

He trailed a hand lightly down her arm. "Let's get out of here."

Poppy hesitated. Once they left the party it would be time to tell him about the baby. She'd put it off long enough.

Before she agreed to leave, Hailey Randall, who Ben had dated last fall, rushed up. "Poppy," she squealed. "Someone told me you were here."

Poppy had always thought of Hailey as Tripp Randall's little sister. But the blonde beauty who hugged her was no child. With a riot of curls tumbling past her shoulders and a cute figure, Hailey was all woman.

"I didn't realize you'd be here, either." Poppy offered the girl a warm smile. "What a nice surprise."

"Mitzi invited me." Hailey gestured with her head to a mountain of a man over by the buffet table. "Rowe plays football with Mitzi's boyfriend, Kelvin. He wanted a date."

Rowe was busily flirting with a redhead that Poppy recognized as a nurse from the hospital.

"How's that going?" Poppy asked.

Hailey's lips twisted. "When I tried to talk about what a speech therapist does, his eyes practically glazed over. But now Leila is telling him about what it's like to work as an RN in obstetrics and he's hanging on every word."

Poppy noted the direction of Rowe's gaze and smiled. "I think his interest is elsewhere."

Hailey shifted her gaze then chuckled when she saw Rowe's gaze fixed on Leila's ample bosom. "Well, he can have her, er, them, if he wants. The big burly focused-on-boobs type doesn't interest me."

The speech pathologist's gaze shifted to Ben. "Hey, stranger. Haven't seen you around."

"I've been busy." To Poppy's horror she felt Ben's hand settle on her waist.

"Oh." Hailey's gaze shifted from Ben to Poppy then back to Ben. "I didn't realize the two of you were...together."

"Actually—" Poppy began but Rowe called to Hailey, motioning her over.

Heaving a melodramatic sigh, the blonde flounced across the room.

Poppy turned to find Ben staring at her. The heat in his gaze made her heart stutter.

"Are you ready to leave?" he asked again.

"I did not hear the word 'leave' come from your lips." Out of nowhere Mitzi appeared, looping her arm through Ben's. The easy familiarity between the two was hard to miss. "Poppy hasn't even had a glass of wine. Neither have you."

"I have an early-morning surgery tomorrow." Ben gently disentangled Mitzi's hand from his arm.

His colleague's brow furrowed. "Tomorrow is Saturday."

"Next week is full," Ben answered even as his arm tightened around Poppy's waist. "This couldn't wait. I had to fit him in."

"In that case, you're excused." Mitzi turned to Poppy. "Make sure he gets his sleep."

Poppy opened her mouth but before she could speak, Mitzi laughed and waved a hand. "What am I thinking? The way he's looking at you, catching a few winks is the last thing on his mind."

Ben merely smiled. "Nice place, Mitz. I'm sure you'll be happy here."

"I believe I will." Mitzi raised herself up on her tiptoes, brushed her lips across his cheek then smiled. "Thanks for coming. You and Poppy have fun."

"Mitzi, where did you put the extra bottles of wine?" Kate Dennes, a local pediatrician and one of Mitzi's closest friends, rushed up.

When Mitzi turned to Kate, Poppy and Ben were able to slip away. Still, they were stopped by various friends several times on their way to the door. Ten minutes later they were finally outside.

Though he didn't touch her as they strolled to his Ben's car, heat raced through Poppy's veins like an out-of-control locomotive. "That was fun."

Ben shot her a look that asked if she'd lost her mind. "It was loud and crowded and...loud."

Her grin came far too easily. "Tell me how you really feel."

"If she wasn't a colleague, I'd have been tempted to blow off the party," he said quite seriously. "Having you there with me made it bearable. Barely."

"Don't give me that." Poppy stepped aside while he opened the car door for her. "You knew everyone. There were any number of women who'd have been happy to keep you from being bored."

With great gentleness, his hand brushed a strand of her hair back from her face. "I'm with the only woman I want to be with tonight."

Her heart stuttered despite her efforts to be unaffected. Smooth. She'd give him that. The guy was smooth.

Ben leaned forward as if to kiss her but she turned her face and slid into the car. The last time they'd been together she'd given in to a desire for this smooth talking doctor and where had it gotten her?

Knocked up.

Ben closed the door firmly then in seconds was behind the wheel. "I don't know about you but I'm starving."

"You could have eaten at the party," she pointed out.

"Too loud." He slanted a sideways glance. "What's your excuse?"

"Too loud works for me." Her retort made him laugh.

Poppy didn't think she could eat if someone force-fed her. A thousand butterflies had invaded her stomach. Should she give him the news now? *No,* she told herself, *not while he's driving.*

Though she planned to tell him tonight, Poppy hadn't thought where the discussion would take place.

Somewhere private, she thought, *yet public. Somewhere I can easily leave if he gets too upset.*

"How does stopping at Perfect Pizza sound?" she asked.

Her apartment was only a short walk from the popular eatery in downtown Jackson.

"Sounds good." Ben turned onto the highway.

"How's Groucho?" Poppy hoped a little more casual conversation would still her nerves.

Ben's quicksilver grin told her all was well with the schnauzer. "He loves this warm weather."

Poppy kept the conversation focused on the dog until they reached the eatery. It was busy, but not too busy for them to snag a booth in the back corner of the dining room.

"Being with you tonight has been...nice." Ben leaned back and studied her. "I've missed you, Poppy. We had one amazing night, then nothing."

"We had a deal," she said simply.

He reached across the tabletop and took her hand. "Yet, here we are."

When his thumb caressed her palm, Poppy couldn't bring herself to pull away.

"There's something I need to tell you," she stammered.

Before she could continue, a teenage boy still in the throes of a war on acne brought out the half pepperoni, half vegetarian pizza. Though Poppy's nausea was mostly confined to morning hours, greasy foods could still surprise her. When they'd ordered, going vegetarian had seemed a sensible choice.

When Ben placed a slice on her plate, simply smelling it caused bile to rise in her throat. She took several deep breaths.

"What's wrong, Poppy?" His brows furrowed in concern. "You haven't been yourself this evening."

"How would you know what I'm like?" Poppy blurted out. "We're strangers."

"I think we're more than strangers." Though confusion filled his eyes, his tone was teasing. "I don't know too many strangers I've seen naked."

Poppy couldn't even muster a smile. "If I knew you better, I'd know the best way to tell you what I need to tell you."

She nearly groaned aloud. *Keep it simple,* she told herself.

Ben's lips curved. He picked up a slice of pizza. "Whatever it is, just say it."

Poppy took a deep breath and looked him straight in the eye. "I'm pregnant."

Chapter Eight

The pizza slid from Ben's fingers to his plate. "Pardon me."

Poppy twisted the paper napkin in her lap, but kept her gaze focused on him. "I'm pregnant," she repeated, as sweat trickled down her spine. "You're the father."

Two lines of concentration formed between Ben's brows. Absently he picked up the pepperoni slice, took a bite then washed it down with soda.

Though she had more to say, Poppy waited. She'd had time to adjust to the fact they'd made a baby. Surely she could give Ben a second or two to mull it over in his head.

"I thought you couldn't get pregnant," he said at last.

"I was wrong." The surge of joy at the realization seemed out of place so Poppy tamped down the emotion.

Ben steepled his fingers beneath his chin. "I assume you had the pregnancy confirmed."

The extent of his control surprised her. She hadn't expected such a rational response. Poppy toyed with her fork. "I took an at-home pregnancy test. Then I saw Travis."

"Travis Fisher."

She nodded again.

"What did he say?"

"The blood test and exam confirmed I'm pregnant." Unconsciously one hand dropped to her flat belly. "The baby is due in November."

Something flickered in the back of Ben's eyes, something she couldn't quite decipher. "Having your suspicions confirmed had to be a shock."

Poppy gave a humorless chuckle, her fingers shredding the paper napkin in her hand. "You, Dr. Campbell, appear to be a master of understatement."

He didn't grin as she expected. Instead, his eyes remained grave. "I'm sorry you had to go to the appointment alone."

Poppy widened her eyes, struck by the gentle kindness in his tone.

"I should have been there with you," she heard him say.

"I didn't know for sure I was pregnant," she stammered. "Until it was confirmed, I didn't want to say anything to you."

"I understand." He reached across the table and surprised Poppy by taking her hand.

The warmth of his touch was so comforting she couldn't make herself pull away. "I thought you might be angry."

"The condom slipped," he reminded her. "I didn't stop. If anyone should be angry it should be you."

Dropping her eyes to the table, Poppy traced a figure eight on the top with the tip of a finger. "Things happen."

"Now we decide where to go from here."

Poppy jerked up her head. "I will continue this pregnancy."

He looked as if she'd punched him in the gut. Still, when he spoke, his voice was even. "Had you considered terminating?"

"Never." Poppy met his gaze. "I simply wanted you to know abortion isn't an option. Neither is adoption."

Ben released a ragged breath. "I'm glad."

The tension gripping Poppy's shoulders eased. Having him push for termination had been her biggest worry. She knew if he tried to shove that option down her throat, her respect for him would plummet.

"I'm fully capable of taking care of this baby on my own." Her voice was steady now. "But I believe a child needs a father as well as a mother. I won't stop you from being involved."

"Stop me from being involved?" The words were cold as polished steel.

"That is, if you want to be involved." She spoke quickly now. "I realize some men don't care to—"

"I'm not some men," Ben snapped, cutting her off. Then he paused. When he spoke again, his voice was once again steady and calm. "This is my child, too, Poppy. I want to be involved. I *will* be involved."

"Oh." She exhaled a ragged breath. "Okay. Good."

He nudged her plate. "Eat."

Poppy gazed down at the pizza, thought about arguing then cut off a piece with her fork and obediently raised it to her lips.

"Do you plan to keep working?"

She swallowed, picked up her glass of milk. "Yes. Of course."

His gray eyes searched hers. "You can move in with me. Angela will ease much of your day-to-day load. And it will give us a—"

"Not an option." Poppy's voice rose and broke. The thought of being under his roof, under his *control,* had panic surging.

Though a muscle in his jaw twitched, Ben effortlessly changed the subject. "What concerned you the most about telling me?"

"I had no idea how you'd react." Poppy embraced the new topic. "I thought you might deny the baby was yours. I want you to know I'm willing to do a paternity test after the baby is born."

He frowned. "You told me you hadn't been with anyone since your divorce."

"I hadn't," she stuttered.

"Have you been with anyone since that night?"

"No," Poppy said, appalled he could think she'd jump from his bed into another. But then she reminded herself they knew so little about each other.

"There's no need for a paternity test." Ben lifted his glass of soda. "Now, tell me why you're so opposed to moving in with me."

Poppy stifled a groan. She should have known he wouldn't accept her refusal so easily. "Because I'm not interested in having a relationship with you."

Ben gave a little laugh but the amusement didn't reach his eyes. "Too late. You and I are going to be parents, Poppy. That means we already have a relationship. For the rest of our child's life, we'll be connected."

"I suppose," Poppy grudgingly admitted.

"This pregnancy took us both by surprise," he said, then waited until she nodded before continuing.

"I believe we owe it to ourselves to take the time to become better acquainted." His tone turned persuasive. "For our sake. For the sake of our baby."

A refusal had been poised on her lips but his obvious sincerity played straight to her heartstrings. Didn't this child she carried, *their* child, deserve the best life possible? In her mind, that meant a mother and a father who worked together.

Ben sat back in his seat. He'd volleyed. The ball was now in her court.

It was a weighty ball. Though Ben had a lovely home, she'd be out of her element there. Everything would be his, including his rules.

It'd be the New York penthouse all over again.

"I can't live in your home."

"It's a good solution, Poppy. We need to get to know each other."

"We can get to know each other without living together."

"Can we?" He raised a brow. Though he appeared perfectly composed, a muscle in his jaw jumped. "We both work long hours. You told me you're in bed by eight. If we're not under the same roof, when would we connect?"

Poppy opened her mouth to speak but he held up a hand.

"If we lived together, we'd at least see each other in the morning and at night." His eyes searched hers. "I've heard you never really know someone until you live with them."

She thought of Bill. Poppy had been adamant about not living with him before they married. If she had, she might have saved herself a whole lot of heartache.

Ben was her baby's father. As her child grew older he—or she—would be spending time alone with him. She had no idea how Ben reacted when he was tired, frustrated or angry. And that certainly wasn't anything she'd be able to discover on weekend "dates" when they'd both be on their best behavior.

Taking a deep breath, Poppy let it out slowly. The welfare of her child, she reminded herself, was all that mattered.

"I won't move in with you, and I don't want to get into some big discussion about my reasons. But you can move in with me," she heard herself say. "My place isn't big but there are two bedrooms."

"Your place," Ben repeated as if actually considering the possibility. After a moment, he nodded. "I'll do it."

Poppy jerked, almost knocking over her milk, reaching out with a shaky hand to steady the glass. "Excuse me?"

"I'll move in with you," he repeated. "Does your complex accept dogs?"

"What? Oh?" Of course, he'd want to bring Groucho. "I'm sorry. My landlord has a no pet rule. Firm."

He puffed out his cheeks then nodded. "He'll stay with my parents."

Impressed despite herself, Poppy could only stare. It was as if Ben had days, weeks, to think this over and come up with a rational plan, instead of mere minutes.

"If it works for you, I'll move in on Sunday."

"Ah, sure," Poppy stumbled over the words. "That'd be fine."

Fine? She resisted, but barely, the urge to fall into hysterical laughter. She was going to spend the next few months living with Ben Campbell.

Then what?

Nervously, she reached for the now shredded napkin then ran her tongue across suddenly dry lips. "You realize this living arrangement is only temporary."

"By the time our baby is born," he said with an easy smile, making no promises, "we'll know each other better. Together, we'll decide where to go from there."

Poppy wanted to tell him she already knew where they'd go from there. He'd go back to his house and his world. She'd regain control of her apartment and her life.

Yes, they'd go back to the way things were before, except for the baby they'd share...for the rest of their lives.

When Ben had asked if he could bring his clothes over at noon, what could Poppy say but yes? Feeling the need for some spiritual solace, she rose early and headed to the church she'd attended as a child.

Though she knew everything was more casual than when she was growing up, Poppy couldn't bring herself to wear jeans. Instead she pulled a bright blue summer dress from her closet along with a pair of strappy sandals.

To jazz up the outfit, she pulled back the hair on both sides of her face, clasping the strands in one of the glittering pins she'd worn during the torch singing competition.

Fussing over what to wear took longer than planned. By

the time Poppy arrived at the small white clapboard church, the pews were almost full. Though Poppy was used to going solo, for some reason it bothered her that everyone seemed to have someone by their side. Everyone but her.

"And just how did you come by that hair clip, missy?"

Poppy whirled. Cassidy stood behind her, small blond spikes tipped with fuchsia jetting out from her head, a big grin on her shockingly bright red lips. The stylist wore jeans and boots with mile-high spiked heels and a sweater that matched the tips of her hair. Long, multicolored earrings dangled from her lobes.

"Was I supposed to give the clips back to you?" Poppy automatically stepped to the side while they talked.

"Just screwing with you." Cassidy laughed.

"It's going to be a full service." Poppy's gaze shifted to the almost full church. "Are you here with anyone?"

Cassidy shook her head.

"Me, either." Poppy forced a bright smile. "We could sit together?"

"That'd be cool," the stylist said in an equally casual tone.

They found a pew toward the back that had just enough room on the end for two and took a seat.

Poppy had just risen for the first hymn when a familiar voice sounded beside her.

"Do you have room for one more?"

When she turned, Poppy's traitorous heart skipped a beat.

Dressed in dark pants and a gray shirt, Ben stood in the aisle, hair still damp from the shower and smelling terrific.

"Absolutely." Cassidy spoke before Poppy could inform him the pew was full. "There's always room for you, Dr. Campbell."

The orthopedic surgeon flashed the hairstylist a devastating smile. "Please, call me Ben."

When she heard Cassidy sigh, Poppy knew Ben had a fan for life. Poppy sighed for a different reason. When they sat down, she knew she'd practically be in Ben's lap.

Since she and Cassidy were sharing the hymnal, Poppy held it midcenter, so Ben could see the words, too. As he leaned close she inhaled the clean fresh scent of him. Instead of lust, a curious type of longing rose up inside her. A wish that somehow he could be different, that she could be different.

Poppy knew the personalities of successful doctors, especially surgeons. It didn't mean she lumped them all in one basket. That would be silly. But she knew the drive it took to succeed, as well as the ego.

She'd had a taste of that kind of man. That taste certainly hadn't left her longing for more. But Ben was in her life, the father of her child. That couldn't be changed.

The hymn ended much too soon. When Poppy sat, Ben's thigh pressed tightly against hers. The only way they could be comfortable was for him to loop an arm around her shoulders, which brought a hum to her blood.

"I didn't know you went to church here," she whispered to him while a skinny woman with poufed hair read a verse from the Bible.

"I don't come that often," he said in an equally low tone. "But today, it felt necessary."

Poppy tried to focus on the woman reading the verse. But all she could think was in a couple hours she and Ben would be under the same roof and both their lives would be thrown into turmoil.

Her entire apartment could fit into his master bedroom. They'd be on top of each other from day one. Unbidden, the image of the last time he'd been on top of her flashed before her.

Poppy slanted a sideways glance. His handsome face made her shiver. A woman exploring her spontaneous side could have some interesting times with such a man.

Especially if they were…on top of each other.

Chapter Nine

The sermon was interesting, but Ben was far too conscious of the beautiful brunette at his side to catch more than a few words. Maybe it was Poppy's perfume, the same sultry scent she'd worn the night they made love. Perhaps it was the feel of her soft hair brushing against his arm whenever she leaned back in the pew. It didn't help that her leg was pressed so tightly against him that his heat mingled with hers.

He wanted Poppy. Conversely, he wanted to get as far from her as possible. All or nothing. He'd never been able to figure out another way to live.

When Kristin left him during his last year of residency, he'd eventually concluded the jolt her leaving had given his heart was partially his fault. He'd let her get too close, given too much of himself to her.

The intensity of his attraction to Poppy told him she could be equally dangerous. Yet, she was pregnant with his baby. He couldn't keep his distance. He needed to get to know the woman who'd be the mother of his son or daughter. He had to stick close.

As he thought of her small apartment, Ben's lips twisted in a wry smile. He doubted staying close would be an issue.

The organ sounded. They stood for the closing hymn, and Poppy held out the book. His fingers brushed hers. Ben cast a sideways glance to see if she felt the searing heat, but she was already singing. By the time the hymn ended, his hand wasn't the only part of his body on fire.

Before he could exit the pew and put physical distance between them, Travis was there. Ben had noticed the doctor, his wife and their five little ones seated several pews up when he'd entered the church.

"We're headed over to The Coffee Pot for breakfast." Travis rocked back on the heels of his cowboy boots. "Thought you might want to join us. It's been a while."

Ben hadn't thought about eating, only about putting some needed distance between him and Poppy. Still, this would be an opportunity for them to be seen publicly as a couple, which should staunch some of the gossip when news of the baby got out.

He slanted a glance at Poppy and raised a brow.

To Ben's surprise she turned to the woman seated on the other side of her. "What do you say, Cass? Hungry?"

The hairstylist's expression brightened. She opened her mouth. Then with apparent reluctance, hesitated. "I'm not sure Dr. Fisher meant to include me."

"Jeez, Cass," Travis snorted. "What's with the Dr. Fisher crap? We went to school together. We used to party together. Of course you're invited."

Cassidy's red lips curved. "Then count me in."

Since The Coffee Pot was only a few blocks from the church, Poppy decided she would walk. She hoped a few minutes of fresh air would clear her mind and settle her nerves. Sitting next to Ben for nearly an hour had taken a hard toll.

Unfortunately when she told him she'd meet him at the café, he told her a little fresh air sounded good to him, too. Not surprisingly, the hairstylist opted to join them.

Cassidy chattered nonstop since taking her first step down the sidewalk in those teetering heels. All Ben had done was ask how she'd gotten started in her business and the hairstylist began spilling her life story.

Well, not exactly her *entire* life story, Poppy noted. Because she herself often skipped her years of marriage, she noticed Cassidy said very little about her childhood. It was as if her life had started after she'd graduated from high school.

"The cost for retail space is outrageous in Jackson." Cassidy heaved a theatrical sigh. "If you don't have the clientele, you don't stay in business long."

"You must be proud to have built such a successful business at such a young age," Ben said with what appeared to be obvious sincerity.

"Lots of people predicted I'd fail." Cassidy gazed up at Ben through lowered lashes, an almost flirtatious gesture. "But I'm very good with my hands."

Poppy's eyes widened but she said nothing.

Cassidy continued to expand on her "talents," seeming to enjoy Ben's interest.

Poppy pretended she was alone. A woman enjoying a stroll on a beautiful April day, the sun warm against her face. With each step, the tension in Poppy's shoulders melted away.

While admiring a cardinal perched atop a parking meter, Poppy realized Cassidy had fallen silent. She refocused on her two companions, favoring the stylist with a smile. "I'm impressed, Cassidy."

Cassidy brought a heavily lacquered purple nail to her

lips and offered a sheepish smile. "I think I've monopolized the conversation."

"Not at all." Poppy wished there was a way to tell her former high school classmate to just keep talking. The alternative was having Cassidy watch and analyze her interaction with Ben.

With an audience, Poppy didn't know how to act, what to say or how much to reveal. And she realized with a sudden jerk, she didn't know what Ben might say. A chill, cold enough to freeze her breath, swept through her.

Would Ben mention he was moving in with her? It was a possibility. If he did, there would be questions, lots of questions. The baby might come up.

Poppy suddenly felt light-headed. With Cassidy there to hear it all, the news would be all over Jackson Hole before the sun went down.

Though she understood her condition would soon be public knowledge, the thought of everyone looking at her, judging her brought tears to her eyes. *Darn hormones.*

"Poppy?" Ben rested a hand on her arm, his tone gentle.

"I need a minute." Thankfully she'd spoken low enough that only he heard the shakiness in her voice.

"Is something wrong?" Cassidy's gaze shifted from her to Ben, those blue eyes reminding Poppy of a ferret catching sight of a mouse.

Poppy forced a wan smile. "I'm just tired. I didn't sleep well last night."

"Cassidy, why don't you go in and let everyone know we'll be a few minutes." Ben may have spoken to the stylist but his gray eyes remained focused on Poppy.

"I'll wait," Cassidy said.

"Okay. But I have something to discuss with Ben first." Poppy wrapped her fingers around his arm and pulled him out of Cassidy's earshot.

His brows drew together as he scanned her face. "Is something wrong?"

"You can't tell anyone at the table about the baby or about you moving in." She deliberately kept her tone soft, sensing Cassidy was tuned in to them.

His back went ramrod straight, but when he spoke his voice was conversational and low. "What's got you worried?"

She lifted one shoulder in a shrug. "I want some time to process all this before everyone starts asking questions."

"They'll know soon enough," he pointed out.

"I realize that." Poppy kept a tight grip on her temper. Feeling so exposed, so raw, so *guilty,* was her issue, not his. "If it comes out today, Cassidy will have the news spread all the way to Idaho before we finish our eggs. I'm not ready for that yet."

Ben shot a brief glance at the blonde, who stood pretending to study the menu in the café window. "My lips are sealed."

"Thanks." Relief flooded her. Impulsively, she gave him a quick hug. She wasn't sure which of them was more surprised by the gesture.

When she stepped back, he took her hand. Automatically she started to pull away but he tightened his grip and smiled.

"There will be talk," he said, his tone barely audible. "It will be less if everyone believes we have a relationship. Even a casual one."

What he said made sense. Poppy left her hand nestled in his, no longer feeling quite so alone.

When they reached Cassidy, the stylist's bright lips lifted in a sly smile. "Glad to see you two made up. But what happened to kiss?"

Poppy's puzzled expression made the stylist laugh.

"Kiss and make up?" Cassidy prompted.

Ben laughed.

Poppy shot him a quelling glance and kept her tone matter-of-fact. "Ben and I hadn't argued. We had some quick business to discuss."

"Whatever you say." Cassidy waved a hand in the air but her tone—and the look in those canny blue eyes—said she didn't believe a word.

Poppy started to insist there was nothing between her and Ben, but realized when it came out that she was pregnant with his baby that kind of comment would only fuel the gossip mill.

As they entered the café and wove their way through the tables, Ben's hand rested lightly on her back. It felt as if they were stopped every few feet by townspeople wanting to say hello to Ben.

Warm greetings were also tossed Cassidy's way. No one called out to Poppy. It was to be expected, she told herself, brushing the hurt aside. She'd been away from Jackson Hole long enough that the large group of friends and acquaintances she'd once had was now a handful.

When they reached the long table at the back of the restaurant, there were still several seats left. With gentlemanly aplomb, Ben pulled out her chair and then Cassidy's.

Poppy was thankful to find herself near Lexi. Lexi's handsome attorney husband, Nick, offered a warm smile of welcome.

"Lexi is home at a more reasonable hour these days and I believe I have you to thank for that change." Cut stylishly short, Nick's dark hair provided the perfect foil to his brilliant blue eyes.

"I don't know about that," Poppy told him, "but I enjoy my job and love working with your wife."

She shifted back in her seat and gestured to Cassidy. "Since you both aren't from here, I'm not sure if you know Cassidy Kaye. She owns the—"

"Clippety Do Dah salon." Lexi leaned forward and gave Cass a welcoming smile. "My girls won't get their hair cut anywhere else. I'm happy you joined us this morning."

As the two were chatting, Joel and Kate Dennes arrived.

Poppy discovered Kate and her daughters also went to Cassidy's salon.

Beneath the table Ben squeezed her hand. "Mission accomplished."

Poppy cocked her head.

He leaned close, his breath tickling her ear. "You made Cassidy feel welcome."

The approval in Ben's voice rolled over her as smooth and easy as warm cream.

"It surprises me to see you this morning, Ben," Tripp said from across the table, and Ben straightened. "You're not usually up this early on Sunday."

"I even made it to church, Randall," Ben shot back with equanimity, "which is more than I can say for you."

With his jeans and chambray shirt, Tripp looked more like one of the cowboys who regularly frequented Wally's Place, a popular watering hole, than the administrator of the local hospital. His blond hair was tousled as if he'd just rolled out of bed and the scruff on his chin looked extra shaggy.

In contrast, his wife, Anna, sat cool and serene wearing a trendy spring dress in mint green with a straw-colored sweater over her shoulders. "It's my fault." The midwife spoke in a soft, melodious voice. "I had a delivery that took until three this morning and Tripp insisted on waiting up for me."

"That's just the kind of husband I am." The smirk on Tripp's lips told everyone that once his wife had arrived home, sleep hadn't been a priority.

The waitress hurried over just as Travis and Mary Karen slid into the last two spots.

"Sorry." Mary Karen exhaled heavily, a harried look on her face. "For some reason our son Ben didn't want us to leave him at Sunday school. He started screaming and would not let up."

"The boy has the most amazing stamina." Travis turned

over his cup and smiled when the waitress filled it with dark, steaming coffee.

Ben was one of their youngest sets of twins, a whirlwind of a child, who already made his three mischievous older brothers look like angels.

"Clearly it has something to do with the name," Poppy mused, slanting a glance in Ben's direction.

"Why, thank you, darlin'." Ben looped a casual arm around her shoulders. "I wasn't sure you'd noticed."

Cassidy whooped.

Heat shot up Poppy's neck.

Everyone laughed.

"The two of you make such a cute couple," Mary Karen, a former RN now turned amateur matchmaker, said with a smile.

"What makes you think we're a couple?" Poppy asked lightly then took a second to order her breakfast.

Mary Karen lifted a hand, her shiny diamond solitaire scattering reflections from the overhead fluorescent light. "Oh, let me count the ways."

Poppy's heart sank as Cassidy straightened in her seat. Though Cass's hands were empty, Poppy could almost see her former classmate pull out a mental pencil and notepad.

Stupid. Stupid. Stupid.

She should have simply ignored Mary Karen's comment or changed the subject.

"I don't know if you're aware, but Poppy will be consulting with my office manager on better ways to reach non-compliant patients," Ben interrupted smoothly.

Because most at the table dealt in one way or another with patients, the questions started flying. As Poppy improvised, Cassidy sat back, a look of disappointment on her face.

After making sure Cassidy wasn't looking, Poppy bumped Ben's shoulder with hers and mouthed her thanks.

When he grinned back, a flood of warmth, soft and sweet, flowed through Poppy's veins.

The food arrived and the conversation turned to upcoming events in Jackson Hole. Rather than trying to dominate the conversation as her ex would have done, Ben seemed content to listen and only occasionally comment.

When someone asked about Mitzi and the NFL player, Ben simply shrugged and said they'd have to ask her whenever she showed up. Poppy concluded that while Mitzi occasionally came for breakfast, she hadn't recently.

Poppy got the feeling Cassidy wouldn't mind lingering and trying to ferret out more information. But most in attendance had to get back to the church to pick up their kids from Sunday school. When those with children rose to leave, so did Poppy and Ben. Reluctantly, so did Cassidy.

"Big day?" the hairstylist asked, her gaze shifting from Ben to Poppy.

"Weekends are always crazy." Poppy kept her tone offhand. "Grocery shopping, apartment cleaning, all the normal stuff."

"What about you?" Cassidy focused those shrewd blue eyes on Ben.

"Grocery shopping, apartment cleaning, normal stuff." He flashed a grin then turned the question back at the stylist. "Is your salon open today?"

"We are." Cassidy glanced at the Mickey Mouse watch on her wrist and yelped. "In less than an hour."

Since they'd left their vehicles in the church parking lot, the three of them walked back, with Ben drawing Cassidy out, just as he'd done on his way over. Poppy couldn't help wondering if all the attention was simply to prevent the stylist from asking more questions he knew Poppy didn't want to answer or if he was interested in Cassidy.

A twinge of something that felt an awful lot like jealousy—but couldn't be—rippled through Poppy.

As easy as it would be for someone to dismiss the flamboyant stylist with the fuchsia tinged hair, there was no denying Cassidy was an attractive woman. She had a cute figure, the face of a pixie and big blue eyes that reminded Poppy of the Wyoming sky on a summer day.

Ben had made it clear he admired her entrepreneurial spirit. Perhaps he liked women who were more…spontaneous. Something told Poppy that her classmate had never been accused of being a killjoy.

For a second, Poppy's heart quivered. Well, if Ben wanted to be with Cassidy—or any other woman—he'd have to wait. As long as he was under her roof, there would be no other women. Once they were alone, she'd make that perfectly clear.

Chapter Ten

Poppy watched out her living room window as Ben's car pulled to a stop at the curb, still embarrassed over their earlier conversation. When she told him he couldn't date or sleep with other women while they were living together, he'd looked at her as if she'd lost her mind. He told her straight out neither of them would date anyone else during their time together.

Abashed, the best she could manage was to mumble something about it being good to have ground rules established early.

The slam of a car door pulled her attention back to the window. She wasn't sure if it was the vehicle itself, the fact that Ben was pulling a suitcase out of the trunk or how good his lean body looked in a pair of jeans that caused the unsettled feeling in the pit of her stomach.

While she may have agreed with the reasons they should be under the same roof, until this moment she hadn't believed he'd go through with it. Poppy had been in his house.

She knew how big and gorgeous it was, knew how small and crowded this would be for him.

The knock at the door had her taking another deep breath. Then she walked over and opened it with a smile. "Welcome."

The deep blue polo he'd paired with the unexpected jeans brought out a hint of blue in his gray eyes. If her baby looked anything like him, he or she would be very lucky indeed.

Ben stepped inside. While he placed the suitcase on the floor, his gaze slid around the interior. It didn't take long because there wasn't that much to see. A living room with only enough space for a sofa, chair and flat screen. A breakfast bar, complete with two matching stools, separated the room from a small kitchen. Down the hall were two bedrooms and one bath.

There was off-street parking but no garages, which had made this past winter especially brutal for Poppy. She'd forgotten what it was like to brush snow off your car while a brisk north wind stung your cheeks and made your eyes water.

"This is nice." Though he sounded sincere she wondered how long he'd had to search before settling on that word.

"The rent was reasonable and it's close to downtown." Though it was a far cry from Madison Avenue, it was her home in a way the penthouse had never been. "I can walk to work and I like the fact I'm not locked in. A lot of the places I checked out required a year's lease. My contract here is month to month."

Realizing she'd begun to babble, Poppy shut her mouth.

"You did a lot of research."

"I'm a planner." Pride seeped into the words. "I like to consider all options and make good careful decisions."

Poppy thought of her impulsive decision to sleep with Ben. "Usually," she added.

He simply smiled and gestured to his suitcase. "Where should I put this?"

"I'll show you to your bedroom." Her heart tripped over itself even as she told herself it hardly mattered if he liked it or not. "We each have our own room but we'll share the bathroom."

His implacable expression didn't waver.

"I bet you never had to share a bathroom with anyone." A nervous laugh escaped her lips as Poppy opened the bedroom door. "Or slept in a space this small."

The room was indeed small, Ben realized. Not even as big as his walk-in closet. But it was neat and clean with darkening shades on the window and a comforter devoid of lace or frills.

Ben expelled the breath he didn't realize he'd been holding. He shifted his gaze to Poppy and realized she was waiting for a reply.

"I was sent to a boarding school back East when I was twelve," he told her. "The room wasn't much bigger than this and there were two of us."

Ben had never understood why his parents would pay all that money to send him to a place where he had to share a room and use a shower down the hall.

Poppy stepped into the room and opened a door next to the desk. "For a man with your extensive wardrobe, this may present a problem."

The closet was a door width wide and about three feet deep. Ben decided he was going to have to rethink the extra suitcases in his trunk. It appeared for this situation, less was definitely better.

He sensed her gaze on his face, caught a glimpse of the worry beneath the smooth mask. It was almost as if she feared he wouldn't like the place. But as much as Ben wasn't looking forward to living under these conditions, he'd been honest when he told Poppy they needed to get to know each other. Not just for themselves but for the sake of the child she carried.

His child.

"It's more than adequate. And the room is—" he started to say nice but changed it at the last second to "—sunny and warm." Ben flipped open the latch on his piece of luggage. "I appreciate you making room for me."

"I have a few things to do in the kitchen," she said. "Give me a shout if you have questions."

Without waiting for his reply, she slipped from the room and left Ben staring down at his open suitcase. He thought he'd only packed essentials, but by the time he'd finished taking everything out, the drawers and closets were full.

Think of it as camping, he told himself. He'd loved going out with his dad and brothers when he'd been a boy. In a tent, there was only so much room. He'd never missed all the other stuff while out in the woods.

Besides, he could always keep extra clothes at the office.

After slipping the now empty bag under the bed, Ben went in search of Poppy. It didn't take long to find her. She sat on the sofa with her feet propped up, her laptop humming as data flashed on the screen.

"What are you doing?" he asked, dropping into the adjacent chair.

"Reviewing case notes on a mom and her two kids. I'm trying to secure housing for them."

"Where are they now?"

"In a shelter." She sighed then leaned back and closed her eyes for a second.

There were shadows beneath the long silky lashes. She should be resting today, recharging for the week ahead.

"They make you work on Sundays?" He tried to keep the anger out of his voice. She was pregnant. Wasn't forty hours a week enough for Teton County?

The irritation on his face must have showed because

Poppy chuckled. Despite the shadows, she looked incredibly beautiful in black pants and a bold geometric black-and-white top.

"I choose to work. So many cases, too little time," she said in a matter-of-fact tone. "Plus I'm new so everything takes me more time, including the paperwork."

Ben had envisioned them sitting on a sofa, getting to know each other better over a glass of wine. Of course, Poppy couldn't have wine, so the imaginary scene already had a fatal flaw.

"If you want to watch television, I can go into my room," she offered. "The noise makes it difficult for me to concentrate."

Ben certainly didn't want to make her run off to her bedroom. She had work that demanded her attention. He glanced at the Patek Philippe watch on his wrist, grimaced and rose to his feet. "I have a few errands to run. Do you have a key?"

She reached into the bag that sat on the coffee table and held out her hand. "I had this made for you yesterday."

Her fingers brushed against his as he took it from her. Just a simple metal object, he thought, odd that receiving a key could feel so intimate.

"I have to pick up Groucho and drop him off at my parents' house." He kept his tone casual, offhand, not wanting to pressure her to come when she was busy. "You could come with me. Meet them."

She shook her head and glanced pointedly at the computer screen. "Work to do."

"I understand." He hid his disappointment with a shrug. "I won't be long."

The door closed firmly behind him.

Coward, she chided herself. Still, how could she face his parents? She suspected he'd told them about the baby. There were bound to be lots of questions.

Unsettled, Poppy rose and began to pace. She'd already made such a mess of things.

Ben had specifically moved in so that they could get better acquainted. Yet, she'd pretended she needed to work. *Coward,* she told herself again. This was their opportunity to talk, learn each other's likes and dislikes and ultimately see how they'd work together as parents of this little life they'd created.

After all, this was his baby, too. What if he decided he wants to share custody?

Poppy put a hand on the counter to steady herself as her knees went weak. In her line of work she'd seen many children who spent three days a week with one parent and four days with the other. That arrangement served the parents' needs, not necessarily the child's who had no place to call home.

Ben seemed like a logical man, she reassured herself. A surgeon had to be logical. Still, doubts and fears spun like a twister in her head.

She had to get out, go for a walk, push down the panic rising like hot molten lava inside her.

Grabbing a jacket, Poppy was outside and down the steps in seconds. With no destination in mind, she strolled the sidewalks of downtown Jackson. Because of the balmy weather, tourists and locals were out in force, enjoying the shops and eateries.

Poppy turned when a car pulled up next to the curb and honked.

Her heart sank. It was Ben and staring out the passenger-side window was Groucho.

She sauntered over, ignoring the guilty flush creeping up her neck.

Ben lifted a brow. "You apparently got your work done?"

"I'm taking a break." Poppy glanced at the dog whose

entire body vibrated in welcome. "You couldn't have gotten all the way out to Willowbrook and back."

"Groucho was at the groomers on Broadway." Ben patted the dog's back. "It didn't seem right to drop him off dirty."

Poppy doubted Groucho had ever been what anyone could consider "dirty." She fingered the dog's red bandanna. "He certainly looks pretty."

Groucho barked and Poppy couldn't help but laugh at the animal's expression. "I think he's offended."

"He's a boy. No boy wants to be called pretty."

"Okay, handsome." Poppy reached a hand inside the car and patted the dog's head.

"Are you certain you can't spare a few minutes to come with us? It's a nice drive and I know my parents would like to meet you."

"You told them I'm pregnant." It was a statement, not a question.

"I had to explain why I needed them to watch Groucho."

Poppy raked a hand through her hair. Even though she'd assumed he'd told them, the realization that the news was out was still distressing. "Oh, Ben. I wish you'd waited."

"They won't say anything until I give them the go-ahead." His tone was matter-of-fact. "Look, you'll have to meet them sometime. They're entertaining tonight, so we'll just say hello, drop off Groucho and leave."

Poppy knew he was right. She would need to meet them and today's short visit would be a perfect opportunity. Besides she could hardly tell him she was too busy when he'd caught her window-shopping. "Okay."

Groucho jumped into the backseat while she slipped into the car.

"See," Ben said as he pulled away from the curb. "A few hours around me and you're already becoming more spontaneous."

She cocked her head. "What are you talking about?"

"The night of the torch singing competition you told me you wanted to be more spontaneous. You didn't plan to see my parents today so agreeing to go qualifies."

"As spontaneous?"

"What else would you call it?"

Foolhardy was the word that popped into Poppy's mind. "Spontaneous works."

Though she had to meet them sometime, Poppy hoped she wouldn't regret her "spontaneous" decision to meet them today.

Chapter Eleven

John and Dori Campbell's house sat on eighty acres outside of Jackson, a spacious log home with a magnificent view of the Tetons. As the sleek Mercedes sped down the lane the home came into brilliant focus.

The car pulled to a stop and an ancient lab sleeping on the porch lumbered to his feet and began to bark. Poppy's heart did a couple of slow rolls when the screen door opened. A tall slender woman with short chestnut hair stepped onto the porch.

Dressed simply in navy pants and a nautical-themed cotton sweater, Ben's mother projected an air of casual elegance. She paused at the edge of the porch, dropping one hand to quiet the barking dog. Before Poppy had a chance to open her door, a man who reminded her of an older version of Ben, joined his wife at the rail.

Poppy had heard stories of the steely-eyed orthopedist, a doctor who made residents and nurses quake with his demands for perfection in every aspect of patient care. Even at a distance, Ben's father exuded a commanding confidence.

Taking a deep breath, Poppy stepped from the car. Ben lifted a hand in welcome before joining Poppy in an all too short trek to his waiting parents.

Tail wagging frantically, Groucho emitted tiny staccato barks and raced up the steps to collapse at the feet of the lab.

"What a nice surprise." His mother offered her hand in a natural, friendly gesture. "You must be Poppy. We've heard so much about you. I'm Dori, Ben's mother."

Poppy found it easy to return the warm smile. She gave the slender hand a firm shake, her gaze lingering on the impressive log structure rising two stories behind them. "You have a lovely home."

Dori beamed. "Thank you. We like it very much."

Ben gestured toward his dad. "This is my father, John Campbell."

"It's a pleasure to meet you, Dr. Campbell," Poppy said politely.

"John, please." Though his gaze remained sharp and assessing, he spoke affably. "It's nice to finally get to meet the woman my son will be moving in with."

Ben's fingers dug into her arm.

On the surface, Poppy's schoolteacher father and Ben's dad couldn't be more different. Yet, something about John reminded Poppy of her father. Not only was she not intimidated by the illustrious Dr. Campbell, she found herself tempted to tease. She stifled the urge, instead offering him an easy smile. "As a matter of fact, Ben moved in today."

"I understand you have an apartment in downtown Jackson," John said. "I'm curious how you got him to abandon his new home for a small, less comfortable environment."

No beating around the bush for this man. Exactly like her dad, she thought.

"John," Dori chided. "Don't start badgering the poor woman the second she steps on the porch."

"Yeah, Dad, at least wait until she's in the house," Ben quipped, but Poppy caught the flash of warning he shot his father.

"You're concerned about your son." Poppy met his father's direct gaze with one of her own. The man might have a reputation for being tough, but she saw worry beneath the steely edge. "I understand."

A muscle in Ben's jaw jumped. When he spoke his tone was ice. "Where I live is my business."

"Of course it is, honey." Dori patted her son's arm, as if this byplay between father and son was nothing new. "I hope you and Poppy have time to stay for a glass of tea. I also have ginger cookies. With buttercream frosting."

Poppy's curiosity must have shown, because Dori smiled. "They're Ben's favorite."

What did it say, Poppy wondered, that she and Ben had made a baby, yet she didn't have a clue what kind of cookies he liked?

"I thought you had guests coming," Ben said.

His mother waved a dismissive hand. "I have everything under control."

Ben rocked back on his heels. "I appreciate the offer, and God knows I hate to turn down cookies, but Poppy and I both have work that needs to be completed today."

Poppy had come with him today with the understanding they wouldn't stay. Now he'd generously paved the way for them to leave without making her the bad guy. But the look of disappointment his mother tried so hard to hide tugged at Poppy's heartstrings.

"We've driven all the way out here," Poppy told Ben. "It seems a shame not to stay for a few minutes."

The flicker of gratitude in Ben's eyes sent a current of warmth rushing through her. When he looped an arm around her shoulders, she didn't pull away.

"Looks like I'll get to try one of those cookies, after all," he said to his mother.

"You and Poppy can have as many as you like." Pleasure filled Dori's eyes. "I had Angela make a double batch."

Before they stepped inside, Ben took a second to introduce Poppy to Huck, the ancient yellow lab whose gentle demeanor reminded her of her parents' dog, Otis. She had no doubt that, like Otis, this animal would be wonderful with children.

For a second, she envisioned her and Ben coming for Sunday dinner at this house, watching their little one play with the dog or sit on Grandma or Grandpa's lap while munching on ginger cookies with buttercream frosting. Then she realized that while that might be their child's reality, it wouldn't be hers.

Poppy swallowed a sigh and let Ben usher her through his parents' home. It was as gorgeous inside as out, with shiny hardwood floors, rustic fixtures and comfortable furniture. The floor-to-ceiling windows flanking the back of the great room gave the interior a sense of openness.

The large stone fireplace with an intriguing wood mantel caught her eye just as a tiny white poodle with a pink rhinestone collar pranced into the room to greet the schnauzer.

"Cece has been looking forward to playing with you," Dori told Groucho then opened the French doors leading to a back deck and shooed both dogs outside.

"Thanks for watching him, Mom." Ben moved to his mother's side and gave her shoulder an affectionate squeeze. "I appreciate it."

"Groucho is a pleasure." Dori turned to her husband. "We love having him. Don't we, John?"

"Most of the time he's no trouble," his father agreed.

Though his dad uttered the words grudgingly, Poppy wasn't fooled. On the porch she'd seen him give the dog a treat from his pocket and a pat when he thought no one was looking.

At Dori's direction, Poppy took a seat on the leather sofa. When Ben sat beside her and took her hand, she stiffened before reminding herself this faux demonstration of affection was necessary.

If she and Ben expected others to believe this baby resulted from an intimate relationship—and not a one-night stand—they had to appear "friendly."

"I'll get the cookies and tea," his mother said over her shoulder as she bustled off.

Seconds later Dori returned carrying a teakwood tray filled with glasses of iced tea and a plate of cookies. After placing the refreshments on the trunk-turned-coffee table, his mother turned to Poppy. "You simply must try one."

Poppy obligingly picked up a cookie from the artfully arranged glass plate. She took a bite, and nearly moaned as the rich taste of ginger blended with the buttery cream of the frosting. "This is…wonderful."

Ben grinned. "You have good taste."

"Of course she does." His mother held out the plate to him. "She picked you, didn't she?"

For an instant, Ben's gaze met Poppy's.

"When Ben stopped out the other day he told us how you met." Dori heaved a sigh. "So romantic."

Poppy took a sip of tea. "Did he?"

Ben shifted in his seat to face Poppy. "I told them how cute you looked in your red glasses with your hair piled into that—"

"Beehive," Poppy filled in, then glanced at Dori. "It was a retro party. I wore '60s attire. Ben looked pretty snazzy in his white suit with bell bottoms. Oh, and we can't forget the gold chain."

"God bless the '80s." His mother's laugh was like a silver bell, pure and clear. "John and I prefer the '60s era for such events. I have a Pocahontas headband and huarache sandals I love to pull out."

Dori turned toward her husband. "Remember when you wore that James Dean inspired outfit to the Pomeroys' party?"

John winced and picked up his glass of tea. "Don't re-mind me."

"Winn Ferris went for the *Rebel Without A Cause* look at the Fisher party," Poppy murmured. "Pulled it off, too. Very impressive."

"Winn planned to maneuver Poppy under the mistletoe with him." Ben's voice held a curious intensity. "I wasn't about to let that happen."

Poppy started to laugh then realized he was serious. "Do you expect me to believe you were the reason we found our-selves under the mistletoe together?"

"I've always been resourceful." He lifted her hand, brush-ing a kiss against her fingers.

His mother sighed and Poppy's heart swelled with an emotion she didn't care to closely examine.

"That party was last fall." John's brows pulled together in puzzlement. "If you were so enamored with each other, why were you still dating other people until recently?"

Ben stiffened. He opened his mouth. Shut it.

"Becoming involved with anyone wasn't high on my pri-ority list." Poppy broke off another bite of cookie.

Dori met Poppy's gaze. "You didn't date anyone else."

Though it was a statement, not a question, it required a response.

Poppy chewed, swallowed. "I didn't want to date. But Ben is almost as stubborn as I am…and extremely persua-sive."

"*More* stubborn." Ben shot her a wink. "I may have gone out on a few dates with other women, but you were the only woman I wanted."

Personally Poppy thought Ben was laying it on a little thick. But then his father seemed like a tough nut, difficult to convince. Even now John continued to study her and Ben as if they were puzzle pieces that didn't quite fit.

"It was like that for me once I met your father." Dori shifted her gaze to her husband. "I didn't want anyone else."

Not sure how to respond to that, Poppy took a sip of the tea Dori handed her. "This is delicious. Tangerine?"

"Mango," Dori announced.

Both men grimaced.

His mother lowered herself to the wide arm of her husband's chair. "Ben mentioned you grew up in Jackson Hole but only recently returned."

"I did." Poppy lifted the cut-glass tumbler to her lips. "I attended college and graduate school out of state then lived and worked in New York City for a number of years."

Dori tilted her head, interest flickering in her blue eyes. "What made you come back?"

Poppy had loved the city where she'd spent so many years. Yet, long before her marriage had crumbled, she'd found herself longing for the clear blue skies of Wyoming and the more intimate lifestyle of Jackson Hole. "This has always been home."

Dori took a sip of tea while one hand affectionately stroked her husband's arm. "Are your parents here?"

"They live in California now, close to my sister and her family." Poppy had briefly considered moving near them. But Jackson Hole was home, not Sacramento.

"What do they think about you being pregnant?" John asked.

Heat rose in Poppy's cheeks, but she kept her tone conversational. "I haven't told them."

"What are you waiting for?"

"John," Dori chided.

The man ignored his wife's censuring look. "Are you hoping my son will do the right thing and propose?"

Ben let out an indignant hiss and started to rise. Poppy grabbed his arm and pulled him back down on the sofa.

"I was married once. The experience isn't something I care to repeat." Poppy met his father's gaze, hoping he'd see in her eyes she spoke the truth. "I'm more than capable of raising a child by myself."

"You're not in this alone." Steel ran through Ben's words. "You won't be raising this child by yourself."

"We'd like to be involved, too." Dori spoke slowly, carefully, as if treading on unstable soil that could give way any second. "I believe a child can't have too much love."

The sincerity in the woman's words touched Poppy's heart. "I want you to be a part of this child's life." Poppy glanced at John. "Both of you."

His mother's bright smile and shiny eyes brought an answering lump to Poppy's throat. After quietly clearing her throat, she put down her glass of tea and made a show of glancing at her watch. "Wow. Look at the time. I really need to get back."

Ben pulled to his feet. "Thanks again for watching Groucho."

"He's a sweet boy," Dori told him then shifted her gaze to Poppy. "I'm so happy you came with Ben today."

A few minutes later, as Ben opened the car door and she slipped inside, Poppy realized she was glad she'd come, too. She waited until they were on the highway and headed back toward Jackson before speaking.

"I enjoyed meeting your parents. Your dad…" Poppy paused, smiled. "He's direct."

"He's a good guy but I admit he can be intense. And blunt," Ben added.

"Direct, intense, blunt." Poppy brought a finger to her lips. "Hmm, those words could describe another man I know."

At his questioning look, she smiled. "First name starts with B. Last name Campbell."

"Guilty," Ben said with a laugh.

"Yet, I like your dad." At Ben's disbelieving look, she chuckled. "I do. He's just like my father."

"God help us all," Ben muttered.

"Your mother is a sweetheart."

"She's the best." He slanted a sideways glance in her direction. "It meant a lot to her that you're open to her being involved."

"I'd like both of your parents to be a part of our child's life." Poppy stopped, realized with a start that she'd referred to the baby as their child instead of hers.

Semantics, she told herself. *Doesn't mean a thing.*

She leaned back, rested her head against the seat and tried to control the fluttering in her stomach. "That story you told your parents was inspired."

"Story?"

"Seeing me across the room at Mary Karen's party." Her lips curved. "Your mom loved the part where you said you'd orchestrated it so I'd kiss you under the mistletoe instead of Winn."

"All true."

"C'mon," she began then stopped at his expression. "You're serious?"

"I am." He spoke without apology. "You captivated me. From the first moment."

Poppy blinked. The fluttering in her stomach increased.

As if sensing her unease, Ben glanced at the time displayed on the dash and changed the subject. "Do you want to stop somewhere? Or shall we eat at home?"

She swallowed hard. Cleared her throat.

"We don't have to take meals together." She could have cheered when her voice came out casual and offhand. During her marriage, she and Bill had come and gone as they pleased. Or rather, Bill had, leaving her to fend for herself most evenings.

"Because of our schedules, it's not always going to be possible but I'd like to try." His gaze searched hers. "The reason we're under the same roof is to get better acquainted, to forge a relationship."

Forge a relationship.

Three simple, but terrifying words. She'd agreed to this arrangement for the sake of the baby. But today, she'd spent far more time thinking about the man sitting beside her than her unborn child.

Her intense physical attraction to Ben worried her. Still, she reassured herself that it was likely the more she got to know him, the less she'd like him. "I guess we could try."

"At least in the evening," Ben said. "Mornings are hectic. I try to be out the door by six."

Poppy wrinkled her nose. "I'll probably be rolling out of bed when you leave."

"You're pregnant. You need your sleep."

The understanding had tears stinging her lids. She didn't expect this consideration from him. Didn't want it. Didn't know what to do with it.

Rain had begun to fall by the time her apartment building came into view. On the sidewalk, a man and his cattle dog picked up the pace as they made their way to a 4x4 parked by the curb. Poppy smiled when the guy let the dog into the vehicle first, before he rounded the front and hopped inside.

She thought of Groucho, remembered how forlorn he'd looked, standing on the porch while they drove away. "I'm sorry my place doesn't take dogs."

With studied nonchalance, Ben lifted one shoulder, as if leaving the animal he'd rescued wasn't a big deal. Poppy knew differently.

"You've given up a lot to move in with me," she continued quietly when he eased the car into a parking space close to the building. "Not only Groucho, but your beautiful home."

No wonder his father had been confused. Ben agreeing to move in with her didn't make sense to her, either.

He flicked off the engine, released his seat belt and shifted to face her. "There's nothing more important than us getting to know each other."

"Agreed."

The words had barely left her lips when Ben framed her face with his hands and kissed her.

"As sweet as buttercream frosting," he murmured.

She should call foul. Make it clear that unless they were with others and playing a part, there would be no touching or kissing.

Instead Poppy grabbed his arm and pulled him back to her. After all, she could be spontaneous, too.

She kissed him longer, harder, deeper. By the time they broke apart, they were both breathing hard.

"There," she said triumphantly, her breath coming in short puffs. "We're even."

His gray eyes glittered. "For now."

Chapter Twelve

On a scale of one to ten, with ten being the best day ever, Poppy concluded Monday was destined not to rise above a two. She had a mountain of paperwork to wade through and, to top off the morning, she'd had to testify on an abuse situation involving a sixteen-month-old. By lunchtime, she was already on overload.

It didn't help she hadn't slept well the night before. His kiss. Her kiss. As they enjoyed a meal of chicken stir-fry, all she could think was how his mouth had felt on hers. They might have ended the night even but by the time she'd closed her bedroom door, her body had been so revved up, all she'd been able to do was lie there and think about getting naked with him.

Spontaneity, she decided, had its downside.

Although Ben had tried to be quiet this morning, she'd heard him get up before the sun rose. He was out the door before she tossed back the covers and swung her feet to the floor.

Poppy told herself she was happy he'd already left. But simply smelling the scent of his soap in the shower brought the longing flooding back. As well as a slight ache in her chest. An ache she didn't understand and didn't want to examine too closely.

She figured all these tangled emotions and feelings had to be the result of surging pregnancy hormones. She could only hope a walk in the fresh air over lunch would clear all thoughts of Ben—and this preoccupation with sex—from her head.

Once outside, her feet clad in sensible canvas shoes, Poppy began to walk briskly. She was making good time on her lunch break when she ran into Hailey Randall on the sidewalk outside Hill of Beans, a popular coffee shop and bistro owned by her high school classmate, Cole Lassiter.

"Poppy." Tripp's younger sister greeted her like a long lost friend. "Are you as desperate for a latte as I am?"

Poppy grinned. Something about the perky blonde with the wide smile always lifted her spirits. "I love a good latte."

"Let's get one then. Unless you have other plans?"

Poppy saw the look of hope on Hailey's face and recalled that like her, the young woman had only recently returned to Jackson Hole. After checking the time, Poppy gestured toward the door. "Lead the way."

They ordered then took the drinks and the salad Poppy hadn't been able to resist to a table by the window.

Poppy stabbed a piece of endive with her fork. "How do you like being back in Jackson Hole?"

Hailey sipped her latte and heaved an appreciative sigh before responding. "I enjoyed going away to school and the year after graduation I spent working as a speech therapist in Denver. But when my dad got so sick and it looked, well, bad for him, I needed to be close."

"How's he doing?"

"Much better." There was no mistaking the relief in Hailey's voice. "A new chemo regimen ended up being an answer to our prayers."

"Now that his health has improved, will you be returning to Denver?"

Hailey appeared to give the question some thought then shook her head. "I didn't realize just how much I missed my family until I came back. I like having dinner with my parents and hanging out with Tripp and Anna. I always wanted a sister. I now have one in Anna."

"The move worked out."

"It did." Hailey took another sip. "Other than I don't have a job. Unless you count being a part-time server at Wally's Place. But I'm a speech pathologist. I want to work in my field."

"Something will turn up."

"I've applied everywhere." A shadow passed over Hailey's pretty face. "I've come close, but they ended up hiring someone with more experience."

"That's tough," Poppy said.

"My mom says everything happens in God's time." Hailey's lips twisted in a wry smile. "I only wish God and I could synchronize our watches."

Poppy understood the frustration in Hailey's voice. "When I moved back, not having a job drove me crazy. You and I are alike in that way."

Hailey nodded and peered over the top of her cup. "There's another way we're alike."

Poppy cocked her head.

"We've both dated Ben Campbell."

Poppy nearly choked on a leaf of lettuce. She took a gulp of the water she'd gotten in addition to the latte. "That's true."

"He's a nice guy, don't you think?"

"Very nice." Poppy paused, considered the best way to tell Hailey that Ben had moved in with her.

"I think he likes you more than me," Hailey said philosophically, "though it appears neither of us have the inside track."

Poppy took a sip of water.

"If we did, we'd be the one he'd asked to lunch." Hailey gestured her head toward the door. "Instead of her."

Poppy swiveled in her chair. Her heart rolled. Standing in line to order was the father of her baby and his one time girlfriend, Mitzi Sanchez.

Ben had never thought of himself as being particularly intuitive. While he had good instincts and a brain made for problem solving, the sixth sense that so many people seemed to have eluded him. Until this moment.

The tiny hairs on the back of his neck tingled and he turned toward the dining area. He spotted Poppy immediately, seated by the window.

He lifted his hand in greeting. Both Poppy and Hailey acknowledged his wave before turning back to each other.

"Who is it?" Mitzi asked. "More importantly, do they have a table big enough for us to sit with them? This place is packed."

"Let's order first." Ben turned back to the counter where Cole Lassiter stood, waiting to take their order.

Cole was a local boy who'd started from nothing to become a successful entrepreneur. His multistate Hill of Beans empire was run out of Jackson Hole. His wife, Meg, was also a successful business owner, having started a physical-therapy clinic several years earlier.

"They trust you to take orders, Lassiter?" Ben joked with an easy smile.

"Keep that up and your order could mysteriously end up in the circular file," Cole said, a wicked gleam in his eyes. "You're looking especially lovely today, Ms. Sanchez."

Ben shifted his gaze. His colleague wore a green dress with boots. She looked nice, he supposed.

Mitzi smiled. "Kelvin tells me your wife is really cracking the whip."

"That's why I suggested he see her for his physical therapy when he's in Jackson," Ben told Mitzi. "Meg gets excellent results."

"I'll pass along the compliment," Cole said, then took their order.

Once they received their food, Ben scanned the crowded dining area. There appeared to be room at Poppy and Hailey's table but he decided to take his food back to the office.

"It's crowded," Ben told Mitzi. "Let's bag this stuff and eat at the clinic."

"Where's your spirit of adventure?" Mitzi's eyes narrowed then lit up. "Unless they're meeting someone, Poppy and Hailey should be able to fit us in at their table."

Without waiting for a response, Mitzi began weaving through the tables.

Ben saw no choice but to follow.

"May we join you?" Mitzi asked, resting her tray on the table.

"Of course," Hailey answered immediately.

"Please, join us," Poppy echoed.

She'd been in bed when he'd left this morning. He didn't think he'd ever seen the red suit she had on with the silky white blouse underneath. It looked good on her. Sexy. Poppy was meant to wear red.

"Mitzi and I were at a continuing education seminar at the hospital this morning and decided to grab something to eat before heading to the clinic." Ben felt compelled to explain, yet not sure why. He and Mitzi were in the same medical practice. There was nothing odd about them having lunch together.

Then why does being with her feel wrong? Ben thought.

"Poppy and I ran into each other outside and decided to grab some lunch," Hailey said.

"I thought you made a sandwich last night." The words were out of his mouth before he considered them.

"I did." Color rose high in Poppy's cheeks. "But I forgot the sack in the refrigerator."

Hailey paid no attention. She was too busy complimenting Mitzi on the necklace with copper strands and brightly colored stones that hung around her neck.

But his colleague never missed a beat. Mitzi was an expert at reading between the lines and delving into the nuances of any situation.

"How did you know she made a sandwich for lunch last night?" Mitzi asked him. "Did she call you up and tell you?"

Hailey gave a snort of laughter.

Poppy stilled, then placed her fork carefully on the table.

"I watched her make it," Ben said with equanimity. "Poppy and I are living together."

Hailey dropped her cup to the table, the hot liquid splashing over the rim.

Mitzi's eyes brightened as if she'd been doing some simple mining and had unexpectedly struck gold.

Poppy gave him a look that said he was going to have a lot of explaining to do tonight.

"Since when?" Mitzi leaned forward, resting her forearms on the table, her eyes skipping between Ben and Poppy.

"Yesterday," Ben told her.

Hailey stared at Poppy, a reproachful look in her eye. "You didn't say a word. You let me go on—"

"I was going to tell you but—" Poppy began, but Hailey had already risen.

"I just remembered somewhere I need to be." Hailey's smile appeared strained. "I'm happy for both of you."

"Hailey," Poppy called out, but the girl disappeared out the front door.

"Looks like she still has a thing for you, Ben." Mitzi took a dainty bite of her egg salad sandwich.

"You're mistaken," Ben said, but a niggle of doubt remained. Though he and Hailey had dated a few times, it hadn't been anything serious. At least, not on his part.

Hailey was a nice woman. They'd laughed and talked and done a little kissing, but that was it. Since Valentine's Day, he'd only seen her once. That was only because he'd run into her downtown and they'd gone to a movie they'd both wanted to see.

He hadn't been lying when he'd told his parents that since last fall the only woman he'd been interested in pursuing had been Poppy.

Poppy sat back down but it was apparent his arrival with Mitzi had ruined her lunch. And he had the feeling that whatever ruined her lunch was going to ruin his, as well.

"So you two are an item." Mitzi's blue eyes sparkled as her gaze shifted from Ben to Poppy. "Spill."

"I'd love to chat but unfortunately I need to get back to work." Poppy flashed a smile that didn't quite reach her eyes. "Enjoy your lunch."

She was quick. Ben would give her that. Poppy was out the door in five seconds flat.

He pushed back his chair with a clatter, keeping his eyes firmly focused on Poppy's bright red jacket.

"I'll see you at the clinic," he said to Mitzi without waiting for a response. He sprinted and reached Poppy as she turned the corner.

"What's the rush?"

"Don't you want to get back to your ex-girlfriend? Or—" Poppy paused "—is she back to current girlfriend status?"

Ben blew out a harsh breath. There were a dozen words he could have said to her, but the hurt underlying the anger in her eyes had him swallowing them whole. When he spoke his tone was matter-of-fact.

"Mitzi is my associate," he said, falling into step beside her. "Nothing more. Whatever we once had is over. It's been over for a long time. We decided to catch some lunch after a CME lecture at the hospital. I didn't mean to interrupt your lunch with Hailey or make you or her uncomfortable."

"You and Hailey dated." Poppy's fingers twisted the handle on her purse. They were headed in the direction of her office but the sedate pace told him she still had time on her lunch hour.

"We did."

"She likes you."

"I like her, too," he said, then quickly added, "as a friend. There was never anything more between us."

The skeptical look on her face almost made him smile. With great restraint, he controlled the urge.

"I never slept with her," he said, though she hadn't asked. "Tripp was on target when he said Hailey was too young for me. We're in different places in our lives. But she's a beautiful, intelligent woman and I enjoyed the time I spent with her."

"I don't think she'd have been quite so upset if you'd made it clear we're not sleeping together, that living together is only a way for us to get to know—"

"That's too much information," Ben interrupted, his tone firm and unyielding. "And no one's business but our own."

"But isn't that lying by omission?"

"What goes on in anyone's bedroom is their business. If they want to assume we're having sex, let them."

"And that's what they'll assume when they find out about the baby." She stopped walking. "I need to speak with Hailey. Though I'm not sure how much to say. What are you going to tell your friends?"

Ben didn't hesitate. He'd given this matter a lot of thought. "That from the first moment I saw you, I couldn't get you out of my mind. That you're pregnant and we're living together now because we really want to give this relationship a shot. For the sake of the baby and for us."

Poppy brought a finger to her lips. "That sounds good. And remarkably sincere."

Ben nodded, his eyes steady on hers. "I figure it's always best to go with the truth."

Poppy told Lexi "the truth" that afternoon.

Her friend's hazel eyes searched hers. "I know about your infertility struggles during your marriage. Discovering you were pregnant had to be both a shock and a great joy."

Poppy glanced at the closed door. The office she and Lexi shared was small, and with the door shut, completely private.

"I wanted a child, but I'd given up on that dream." Poppy remembered the terror—and yes, the unmitigated joy—when she'd gazed down at that thin blue line. "It's a miracle."

"How does Ben see it?" Lexi asked in a tone that seemed a little too casual.

"Are you asking if he blames me or somehow thinks this is my fault?"

"Does he?"

"No," Poppy said, and realized it was true. "It wasn't his fault and it wasn't mine. It's almost as if…"

"As if," Lexi prompted when Poppy didn't continue.

"As if this child was meant to be. I find myself lying there at night, thinking there's a child growing inside me and I'm so happy. Then I feel guilty for feeling so much joy."

"Why? Because this baby was unplanned? Because you and Ben aren't married and are just starting a relationship?" Lexi gave Poppy's hands a squeeze. "You want this baby. You'll be a wonderful mother. That's what matters."

Heat rose up Poppy's neck. "It just seems ironic that we counsel our clients on having safe, responsible sex and I turned up unmarried and pregnant."

"Your personal life isn't their business," Lexi asserted. "And having an unplanned pregnancy, despite taking all the precautions, will make you more empathetic to those who find themselves in similar situations. I know raising a child as a single parent helps me to understand better what that's like for our clients."

"Single parent?" Poppy had met Lexi's husband and their two daughters.

"Addie's father and I never married." Lexi gave a little laugh. "I got pregnant in graduate school. My boyfriend and I had been planning to get married so I thought we'd just reschedule the wedding day."

"I take it that didn't happen."

"Drew wasn't ready to be a father. He wanted us to travel, enjoy a child-free life before getting tied down. The timing just wasn't right for him."

A sick feeling filled the pit of Poppy's stomach. "What happened?"

"He made it clear if I didn't terminate the pregnancy we were done." Lexi lifted one shoulder. "He didn't even acknowledge Addie existed for the first ten years of her life. No child support. No visitation."

"Jerk."

Lexi just smiled. "Then I met Nick. When we married he became Addie's dad. Drew eventually came around and now Addie has two fathers."

"Why didn't you tell him to take a flying leap when he came around after all that time?"

"The thought crossed my mind." Lexi toyed with a pencil in need of a good sharpening. "But Nick reminded me it was about what was best for the child. Having Addie get to know Drew and forgive him was what was best for her."

Poppy pondered Lexi's words on her way home. *What was best for the child.*

That was the reason she'd let Ben move in with her. She expelled a breath. All the second-guessing she'd done over her decision disappeared.

She needed to put more effort into developing a relationship with Ben, one that would allow them to effectively parent their child.

Ultimately that's what was important.

Chapter Thirteen

Ben arrived home, or rather to the small five rooms he now called home, shortly before six. The moment he opened the door his senses were assailed by the scent of spiced meat. He found Poppy at the stove stirring what looked to be a pot of vegetables.

"Something smells good," he said, collapsing into a chair in the living room.

"Beef stew." Poppy turned to him. "Please tell me you're not opposed to red meat."

He grinned. "Eat it every chance I get."

She looked so pretty standing at the stove with the red glasses perched on her nose, dressed in a pair of jeans and a bright blue long-sleeved cotton shirt. He had to resist the urge to sneak up and press a kiss on the back of her neck.

"I'll set the table." He glanced dubiously at the surface the size of a postage stamp.

"Thanks." She gestured to a cabinet to her left. "There

are soup bowls in there and plates. I've got biscuits in the oven."

As he took the bowls from the cupboard, his stomach growled. "You didn't have to expend all this effort. If you'd called, I could have picked up some takeout."

Poppy's smile remained pleasant. "I like to cook. After working all day, I enjoy puttering around the kitchen."

"What else can I do?" he asked, dropping napkins next to the dishes.

"I cook. You clean."

"Deal."

Once the food was on the table and Ben had taken his first bite, he realized if he could eat like this every night, he'd never want to go out.

"This is amazing," he said and was rewarded with a bright smile.

"I told Lexi I'm pregnant," Poppy said in an offhand tone and nibbled on a biscuit.

He paused, the spoonful of stew paused in front of his mouth. "What did she say?"

"She…understood." Poppy paused as if deciding how much to confide. "She told me she'd gotten pregnant during grad school and her longtime boyfriend wanted her to have an abortion. She refused."

Ben chased the stew with milk. "Did she keep the baby?"

"It's Addie," Poppy told him. "You've seen her. She's a young teen now and the spitting image of Lexi."

When he lifted a biscuit and took a bite, Poppy took a breath and pressed ahead. "Be honest. When I told you I was pregnant, did you ever consider suggesting an abortion?"

"Not for one second." Ben had been more concerned she might entertain the idea.

"Okay." She expelled a breath and resumed eating. "I've been doing some thinking."

"Thinking is usually good."

She surprised him with a quick smile.

"I really want us to get to know each other," she said. "Start over."

Ben thought that was the reason he'd moved in. "Start over how?"

"By not only getting to know each other but focus on becoming friends."

She looked so intense, so serious, he had to smile.

"I'd like that." He extended his hand, and when she placed hers in his, he realized *now* they had a deal.

Becoming better friends was what Ben had in mind when he asked Poppy to attend a formal hospital function at the Spring Gulch Country Club the following weekend. The fact she'd immediately accepted his invitation had pleased him.

After a hectic week, the night arrived. Ben wandered into the living room, buttoning the cuffs of his shirt. His pants and jacket lay over the top of the sofa. He supposed he could have dressed in his bedroom, but the area was so small, it made him feel as if he was dressing in a closet. He dumped his shoes on the floor.

"I'm sorry."

He turned to find Poppy looking oddly flustered. "I didn't know you were getting dressed in here."

"Nothing here you haven't seen before," he reminded her, flashing a smile.

For tonight's festivities, she wore a silky looking dress in an eye-popping red and shiny black heels that added three inches to her height. He liked her in red, he decided, recalling the suit she'd worn earlier in the week.

"Very pretty," he said after giving her a thorough appraisal. "You'll definitely be the most beautiful woman in the ballroom this evening."

She blushed again.

"I have to do something with my hair." Even as a hand rose to her dark, silky strands, her gaze lingered where his shirt tails ended and his boxers began.

Heat surged through his body but he forced himself to ignore it. He studied her hair, which hung loose to her shoulders in soft curls. "Why do anything with it?"

"It's too plain." She pulled her brows together then brightened. "I have a glittery red headband that might add some pizzazz."

He could honestly argue she didn't need any adornment, but in the past week he'd learned that Poppy didn't go out of the house unless she looked, well, perfect.

"Get it." He reached for his trousers. "I'll give you my opinion."

By the time she returned he was pulling on the jacket of his black tux.

Thin as a pencil width, the "headband" sparkled prettily against her dark hair.

He tilted his head back. "You're right. I like the effect."

She smiled, then sobered. "I'm excited about the party but in some ways I wish we could stay home, have pizza and watch a movie."

Ben almost reminded her that's what they'd done last night, when he caught the tension on her face. "You're nervous. Why?"

She took a deep breath, let it out slowly. "You told Tripp about the baby."

"You told Lexi."

"I know." She brushed at her hair with her hand and the brightly colored stones on her bracelet shimmered in the light. "I guess I'm still embarrassed."

He straightened the sleeves of his jacket and waited.

"You know, like back in high school, when you got a hickey on your neck and you worried everyone would see it and know what you'd been doing."

A hickey? It took everything Ben had not to smile. "I have no doubt every one of our friends who'll be at the party tonight had sex before they were married. And hopefully they enjoyed it as much as we did."

A ghost of a smile flickered on her glossy red lips.

"In fact, many of them were on the road to having a family before they were married." When his hand cupped her cheek, she didn't pull away. "No one will judge us, Poppy. If they do, they aren't friends."

With the sultry scent of her perfume teasing his nostrils, Ben gave in to impulse and pressed his lips against hers in a gentle kiss. He leaned forward, resting his cheek against her hair. "Decide to have a good time tonight, and you will."

"You asked what was on my mind. That's the only reason I told you." Her head jerked up. "I'm not a whiner. Or a killjoy."

It was an odd response, he thought, filing it away for future dissection when there was more time.

"You're not, no." He stroked her hair, pleased she didn't pull away. "I want you to always be honest with me."

"I appreciate you taking the time to listen," she murmured against his shirtfront.

"That's what friendship is all about. And I have a feeling we're going to become good friends, Poppy. Really good friends."

Poppy rested her head against Ben's chest while the band played a romantic dance number from the 1940s. As he whirled her across the dance floor Poppy did her best to ignore the desires his closeness ignited by focusing on the flowers.

The ballroom of the Spring Gulch Country Club had been turned into a wonderland of wildflowers. Large urns overflowed with spikes of red and smatterings of yellow, orange and purples, which filled the room not only with color, but with a sweet, enticing fragrance. Women in brightly colored dresses added their own touch to the ambience.

Poppy spotted Hailey in a short electric blue dress, laughing with Tripp and Anna. Since her brother was the hospital CEO and her father had served several terms on the board of trustees, it was only natural the pretty blonde would be in attendance.

Though Poppy had left a number of messages for Hailey and had even stopped at Wally's Place one afternoon, they'd yet to connect. A crowded ballroom with people surrounding them hardly seemed the time or place to clear the air.

Besides, Poppy was determined to have a good time tonight. So far, so good. Ben had been an attentive "date," getting her a glass of club soda, including her in conversations when various colleagues paused to chat. Yes, she was having fun.

There was still dinner to navigate. Because it was assigned seating, she had no idea who'd be at her table. Of course, it couldn't be any worse than when Lyle Stockwood, one of her husband's associates, had sat beside her and slid his hand up her thigh. When she'd told Bill, he'd had the audacity to laugh and tell her to loosen up.

Dread filled her stomach when Tripp announced it was time for everyone to take their seats. She and Ben located their name cards on a large round linen-clad table near the front.

Poppy immediately checked out the other names. Ryan and Betsy Harcourt. Cole and Meg Lassiter. Tripp and Anna Randall.

She'd attended Jackson Hole High with everyone except Betsy Harcourt. But when Ryan walked up with his wife, Poppy recognized the woman dressed in a flirty bronze-colored dress. Betsy had been a friend of her sister Aimee's.

"It's good to see you both," Ryan said as he shook Ben's hand then smiled at Poppy. "I don't know if you've met my wife, Betsy."

Before Ryan had a chance to complete the introductions, Betsy jumped in.

"You're Aimee's sister, right?" Betsy's freckled face grew animated. "I'm sure you don't remember me but she and I used to hang around together."

"Of course I remember." Poppy had always liked Aimee's shy friend. "You two worked on that science project in middle school."

Betsy grimaced. "Yes, well, just know that I hold myself personally responsible for the drop in her GPA that semester. Aimee was brilliant, but science was always a struggle for me. What's she doing now?"

Poppy told her Aimee was a design engineer, who now lived in Sacramento with her husband and two children. She learned Ryan and Betsy had a little boy who would turn one in the fall.

Cole and Meg strolled up with Tripp and Anna. As the conversation swirled around her, Poppy realized she knew those at the table even better than Ben. Or at least their history. It was easy to forget Ben's parents had sent him off to boarding school at twelve. He hadn't been part of their high school crowd.

"It sounds as if it's really going to happen," Meg said to Betsy, her voice shaking with excitement. "I bet you're so excited."

With her auburn hair, freckles and lean frame, Meg was more striking than pretty. Yet there was something about her that drew people to her, that made them feel comfortable around her.

Though Betsy and Meg were talking quite openly across the table, Poppy wasn't sure if this was a private or a public conversation. She took a bite of salad and chased it with a sip of water.

Ben was busy discussing investment strategies with Cole while Anna and Tripp chatted with Ryan.

"We believe he'll be out of prison by Christmas," Betsy said.

"Prison?" The word popped out before Poppy could stop it. "Who's in prison?"

"My brother, Keenan." Betsy swiveled in her seat toward Poppy. "He was unjustly convicted of murder. The person who set up the killing needed a scapegoat. My brother was in the wrong place at the wrong time."

"I remember Keenan." Poppy slanted a sideways glance at Cole then at Ryan, his two best high school buddies. "I guess I knew he wasn't in Jackson Hole, but I didn't realize he was incarcerated."

"We're hoping he'll be released by Christmas. Maybe even sooner." Happiness laced through Betsy's words like a pretty ribbon.

"I asked Keenan to a turnabout dance in middle school," Poppy said, then heaved an exaggerated sigh. "He turned me down. He was nice about it, though."

"He probably didn't have anything to wear," Betsy said in a matter-of-fact tone. "Until he was old enough to work, there was no money for extras."

Poppy gave a shrug. "I assumed I wasn't his type."

"He'd be happy you didn't suspect money was an issue," Betsy said. "The last thing either of us wanted was anyone's pity."

Poppy placed her hand on Betsy's arm. "Please let him know I'm pulling for him."

"Who?" Ben asked. Apparently derivatives could only hold a man's interest for so long.

"Keenan, Betsy's brother, might be getting out of prison soon," Poppy told Ben. "He got sent there for a crime he didn't commit. I had a huge crush on him in middle school."

"I had the biggest crush on Tripp in middle school. For that matter in high school, too." Anna Randall spoke for the first time. "He didn't know I existed."

"I did, too," Tripp said with a halfhearted protest.

"It's okay." Anna slipped her arm through his and brushed her lips against his cheek, then gently wiped off the lipstick with her fingertip.

Tripp captured her hand and brought it to his mouth.

Observing the sweet, intimate gesture, Poppy's heart twisted. Tripp had dated her dearest friend, Gayle, all through high school. They'd married after college but their happiness had been short-lived. Gayle had died from pregnancy complications four years ago.

"Did you have a steady boyfriend in high school?"

Ben's question pulled Poppy's attention back to him. She shook her head. "I dated a lot but no one seriously. That was deliberate."

"Really?" Curiosity blanketed Meg's face.

"I wanted to go away to college then live in a big city. Getting serious so young would have put a chink in my plan."

"You were married, right?" Betsy asked.

Poppy nodded. "My divorce was final a couple of years ago."

"I heard a rumor." Anna's cheeks turned a dusky pink and she appeared to be deliberately avoiding her husband's gaze. "Are you and Ben living together?"

There were times when it was possible to have a private discussion even when surrounded by people. This wasn't one of those times.

Anna's question had been delivered at the exact moment of a conversational lull. All eyes turned to Poppy.

Beneath the table Ben took her hand. She darted a glance sideways and the look in his eyes told her he was willing to answer the question and take the heat off her.

She shook her head ever so slightly and smiled at Anna. "Ben moved in with me last week."

"You moved into *her* place?" Tripp's tone was clearly disbelieving. "You said you were living together, but I thought, well, you have that beautiful new home in Willowbrook, so I assumed—"

"Assumptions are never a good idea, Randall." Cole Lassiter grunted when his wife elbowed him in the side.

"It doesn't make sense," Tripp said, now flustered.

Before Poppy could respond, Ben's lips lifted in a smile. "We like to keep it cozy."

"Ah, that's so sweet." Betsy heaved a sigh.

"Good for you," Meg added.

"Now, when the baby comes—" Ben began, but that was as far as he got before both he and Poppy were peppered with questions followed by hearty congratulations.

Thankfully, the lights soon dimmed. The video presentation about the assortment of obstetrical equipment tonight's event would fund began. Blessed silence fell over the table. Poppy felt the last of her tension slip away.

Tonight had gone far better than she'd envisioned. Ben had been an excellent companion, solicitous without being stifling. His arm rested against hers as he'd swiveled in his chair to better view the film.

She inhaled the spicy scent of his cologne. He caught her staring and smiled, tucking her hand in the crook of his arm before refocusing on the movie. The longing that rose inside her nearly swamped her with its intensity. How Poppy wished she could forget her reservations and embrace the possibilities of a full and rich relationship with Ben.

But emotion had led her into a marriage with a man who was all wrong for her. Though Ben wasn't an arrogant jerk, he had a healthy ego and a strong personality. *Been there. Done that,* she thought.

Still, becoming friends with the man beside her was her priority. She had seven months to get to know Ben and for him to get to know her.

With a firm foundation built on mutual respect and trust, they'd figure out the best way to co-parent this child they'd created. Then they could both get on with their lives.

"That went well." Ben dropped the car keys on the table inside the apartment's door and collapsed on the sofa.

Poppy took a seat beside him and slipped off her shoes. During the evening the mile high heels, which had been super comfortable in the boutique, had morphed into instruments of torture. She massaged her arch. "Everyone took the news about the baby in stride."

"Lots of congratulations," he agreed.

Poppy slanted a sideways glance. "I thought we might run across your parents."

"Bob and Linda, their friends in Idaho City, are celebrating one of those milestone anniversaries." Unexpectedly he pulled her feet into his lap.

"Hey," she protested. "What are you doing?"

"What does it look like?" He gently stretched the foot up and down while the other hand cupped and supported the heel. "I'm giving you a foot massage."

Sitting on the sofa with Ben felt oddly intimate, especially with his large, skillful hands working their magic.

For a fraction of a second Poppy considered calling a halt, but then he squeezed her foot with both of his hands and the feelings of absolute pleasure wouldn't allow her to act so foolishly.

"You have fabulous hands." Her body shuddered.

"I believe you mentioned that several times the night we spent together," he said with a wicked smile.

"I have a vague recollection of that," she said, stifling a moan when his thumbs stroked the bottom of her foot.

"After I finish, I could give you a repeat demonstration of how versatile these hands can be."

"Very funny."

"The offer remains on the table."

"I'll keep it in mind," she murmured, then released a moan as he found the sweet spot, er, the grooves between the bones and tendons, and stroked with firm pressure.

"Tell me about your parents."

For a second Poppy widened her eyes, not sure she'd heard correctly. "What do you want to know about them?"

"Start with your relationship with your mother. Are you close?"

"We're very alike." Poppy puffed out her cheeks then released the air. "That's why my mom and I clash. Aimee has my father's personality. I have to admit that sometimes I'm jealous of the easy relationship my mom has with my sister."

His hand ran gently up her calf, leaving sparks of heat on the skin. "When I meet your mother, what will be my impression?"

"She's a woman with strong opinions of right and wrong." Concentrating on the question became increasingly difficult as he continued to stroke the bottom of her foot. "My mom has a loving heart but can be pigheaded. Though she likes to laugh and have fun, she's mostly serious. Oh, and she refuses to go out of the house without being perfectly put together."

"And you're like her."

"All but the pigheaded part," she said and made him laugh.

"What are your plans for tomorrow?"

In the fervent hope of prolonging the massage, Poppy had planned to also tell him about her father and sister. But apparently he'd lost interest in her family.

Poppy rested her head against the back of the sofa. "Laundry. Some cleaning. What about you?"

"It's supposed to be unseasonably warm."

"That's a weather forecast, not an answer."

"I thought about picking up Groucho and having a picnic."

"You and Groucho?"

He laughed, a deep heartfelt laugh. "You. Me. Groucho."

"A picnic." Poppy frowned. "Would I have to sit on the ground?"

Ben grinned then gave her foot a quick squeeze. "That's up to you. But sometimes getting down and dirty can be a lot of fun."

Chapter Fourteen

The instant Poppy opened her eyes the next morning, a scratchy pain in her right eye had her turning from the light. She didn't need a doctor to tell her she'd scratched her cornea. Again.

She grabbed the lubricating eye drops from the bedside and bathed her sore eye in the comforting liquid. The contact lenses would remain in the case for today.

Great. Just great.

Pushing back the covers, Poppy swung her feet over the side of the bed and, after grabbing a robe, padded barefoot into the kitchen. She saw the note on the table. After putting on her glasses, Poppy read it before she headed for the shower.

Her mother called before she reached the bathroom and a conversation Poppy thought would last five minutes ended up pushing twenty. Still, she was dressed and sipping a cup of decaffeinated herbal tea when she heard the key in the door. Seconds later, Groucho burst like a bullet into the room. His tail wagged wildly as he zigzagged, checking out the room.

Ben wore jeans, a long-sleeved cotton shirt and boots. It should be a crime for a man to look so sexy this early in the morning.

"Help yourself to coffee." Poppy gestured toward the kitchen counter.

"Thanks."

One word shouldn't tell her anything. Especially one word said from someone she barely knew. But it did. "How were your parents?"

She felt rather than saw his shoulders stiffen.

"Fine," he said.

While she knew Ben well enough to see something had upset him, she didn't have a clue how to proceed. Should she wait for him to tell her what was troubling him? Or did he need encouragement to share?

Perhaps his confidences would come more easily if she did a little sharing of her own. Poppy walked to the tiny window that overlooked the parking lot. For several seconds she stood, letting the sun heat her face. "My mother called this morning."

Out of the corner of her eye she saw him turn to face her, a ceramic mug filled with coffee in his hand. "How is she?"

Poppy turned. The smile on her lips wobbled. "Disappointed."

His gray eyes sharpened. "You told her you were pregnant."

A sip of tea bought her time. "She mentioned she and Dad wouldn't be able to come to Jackson until the fall. That meant I wasn't going to be able to tell them in person. If I had vacation time, I could go to Sacramento for a few days, but I don't."

He took a step closer then stopped. "She had to know how much you wanted a baby. How you thought you'd never have one."

"That's what I'd hoped." To her horror, Poppy's eyes filled with tears.

Before she could blink them back, Ben moved to her, drew her in with his free arm and held her. She let her head rest against the broad chest, drawing comfort from him.

When she'd regained her composure, Poppy lifted her head. "I guess we can't always be the person our parents want us to be."

His smile was rueful. "You can say that again."

She stepped from his arms and studied him. "Your parents?"

"My dad." Ben pressed his lips together, his eyes like ice. "He's a traditional guy."

Poppy gave a strangled laugh. "Which I'm guessing translates to, why aren't you marrying the woman you knocked up?"

"That's pretty much the gist of it," he admitted. "Though he did make it clear he likes you very much."

That made Poppy feel slightly less angry with John Campbell for making his son feel bad. "Did you tell him I wouldn't marry you even if you asked?"

"I told him," Ben began, then paused for emphasis, "it wasn't any of his business."

"I tried that on my mother." Poppy gave a humorless chuckle. "Didn't go over well."

He took a gulp of coffee. "The day will get better."

"I'm not so sure. I scratched my cornea. Now I have to wear these." Poppy tapped her index finger on the rim.

"I like you in glasses," Ben said.

At her grimace, an amused look replaced the somberness in his eyes.

Poppy almost felt better. Then she remembered the disappointment in her mother's voice. The long silence after she'd learned no wedding was planned. She raked a frustrated hand through her hair. "I need air. I'm going for a walk."

Groucho jumped to his feet and let out a single bark.

Poppy scooped up her house key, then paused. "What's up with him?"

"He heard the 'W' word."

"W?"

Ben smiled. "Walk."

The dog leaped in the air, a high whine emanating from his throat. He resumed sitting when Ben motioned him down with a hand gesture.

"Groucho can come," Poppy said.

"What about me?" Ben shot her the same engaging smile that had gotten under her guard on Valentine's Day.

And just like that night, Poppy found the combination of confident charm with a hint of uncertainty impossible to resist.

Poppy lifted a shoulder in what she hoped was an "it doesn't matter to me" gesture. "Up to you."

His smile broadened and he reached for the leash.

Ben couldn't recall what he and Poppy talked about on their walk to the National Elk Refuge, other than it had nothing to do with her mother or his dad. He was hyperconscious of her, the way her green eyes sparkled behind the lenses of her pretty red glasses, how she reached down to affectionately pat Groucho and the way his body responded when his arm brushed against hers.

What they did speak about had little substance. Still, it was enough for Ben to realize Poppy Westover cared deeply about a great many things.

It would have been difficult for a woman with such emotional depth to discover she'd married a man who didn't respect his marriage vows.

He'd been lucky Kristin had called it quits before they'd walked down the aisle. It had been a real kick in the gut when she'd married a fellow resident barely three months later.

While his attraction—and respect—for Poppy deepened

every day, he wasn't concerned about losing his head this time. He wouldn't make the mistake of loving a woman without reservation again.

"I needed this," he heard Poppy say.

He slanted a questioning glance in her direction.

She gestured toward the blue sky, clear but for a few wispy clouds. "This is what I needed to clear my head of the garbage."

"I'm still angry with my father," Ben admitted.

Poppy laid a hand gently on his arm and made an encouraging noise.

"I didn't appreciate being dressed down like an errant schoolboy."

"I bet not." Poppy sighed. "I guess no matter how old we are, we're still their little boy or little girl."

"A frightening thought."

She laughed. "I wonder if that's how we'll be with Jack or Jill."

"Jack or Jill?"

"I get tired of calling him or her 'the baby,'" she admitted. "I can't wait until we know whether we're having a boy or girl so we can start calling him or her by name."

"Leroy," he said. "And if it's a girl, Mabel."

Her eyes flew open. He could practically see the wheels turning in her head as she tried to summon up a tactful response.

He shot her a wink. "Just kidding."

Relief blanketed her face. "You came up with them so quickly, I worried you might be serious."

"Those were the names of two of the dogs I had growing up."

"Cute."

"Not really."

"Seriously, do you have any names that you particularly like? Or family names?"

Ben shook his head. "What about you?"

"I'd prefer to steer clear of the cutesy."

He lifted a questioning brow.

"Such as Poppy." She rolled her eyes. "Honestly, I don't know what my mother was thinking."

"I like your name. It's different and it fits."

"Thank you." She heaved a sigh. "But cute is off the table."

"So we've eliminated Leroy, Mabel and anything cute," he said with a smile. "We're well on our way to finding the perfect name for our child."

Her lips pressed together. "That's what I think irritated me most of all when I spoke with my mother."

Ben opened the gate leading to the refuge and motioned her through.

"She seemed to have forgotten there is an innocent child at the heart of all of this," Poppy continued. "A child I already love. A little boy or girl who'll bring joy into my life. Into my parents' lives, too. That's what my mom should be focusing on, instead of how I disappointed her by getting pregnant without being married."

"We should hook your mother up with my father."

"They'd probably spend the whole time trying to figure out who was most to blame."

Ben chuckled.

"I don't know if I told you this before," Poppy said as they wound their way down a dusty path. "I was fully prepared for you to want to have nothing to do with me when I told you I was pregnant."

Irritation surged. For a second. "That just shows how little you knew me."

"I guess," she said with a shrug.

"And that's why we're now living under the same roof," he reminded her. "To get to know each other."

"Though I now see the value, you had to know I wasn't keen on the idea."

"I got that," Ben said. "But why?"

"While I'm strongly attracted to you physically, you're not the kind of man I could love."

He wasn't the kind of man she could ever love.

Ben slammed the tennis ball back across the net, his mouth set in a hard line, then shifted his stance as Tripp returned the serve.

They volleyed, playing hard as they were evenly matched. Finally a backhanded return that barely skimmed the net then whizzed past Tripp's head only to drop just inside gave Ben the winning point.

They met at the net, sweat streaming down their face, then headed to the showers. By the time they were sitting on the outside terrace of the Country Club with a cold brew and a basket of munchies in the center of the table, Ben's anger had dissipated and once again all he was left with was confusion.

He'd been on that roller coaster the past four days. Ben couldn't believe she could so easily dismiss him as unsuitable.

"How's apartment living?" Tripp asked.

Ben took a long pull from his bottle of beer. "There are worse things than being in close confines with a beautiful woman."

"True." Tripp grinned then sobered. "Everything okay?"

"What could be wrong?"

"You tell me."

Ben simply stared.

"You about took my head off with several of those shots. Anna is tied up with a delivery so I have an excuse for not hurrying home. What's yours?"

"I'm not married," Ben snapped. "I don't have to give Poppy an account of my whereabouts."

Tripp's eyes grew sharp and assessing. "I've known Poppy a long time."

"So."

"I knew her ex." Tripp's lip curled slightly. "Gayle and I used to go out with them about once a month. She was so in love with the guy it made her stupid."

If anyone could understand loving too hard or too much, it'd be him. Empathy welled up inside Ben. "I'm not sure Poppy would be happy to hear you call her stupid."

"I know for a fact she was hard on herself for believing his lies, for failing to see what was right in front of her all those years. But I have to say he was a slick one. Oozed charm."

"She never suspected." Ben said it as a statement, not a question.

Tripp shook his head. "Poppy is a trusting person. She just put that trust in the wrong man."

"I remind her of him, I think."

The hospital CEO gave a hoot of laughter. "You?" He shook his head. "You're nothing like Bill."

Ben gave a slight shrug and took a handful of the snack mixture, wishing he'd kept his mouth shut.

"The whole experience made her gun-shy." Tripp's tone was matter-of-fact. "She no longer trusts her judgment."

Before Ben could respond, Tripp changed the subject to the upcoming Taste of Jackson Hole event. While he listened to Tripp talk about the wine tasting expert who was coming this year, his mind considered Tripp's assessment.

Could it be as simple as her being gun-shy? He knew the sexual attraction that sizzled between them wasn't one-sided. She'd never have hopped into bed with him if she hadn't been drawn to him.

How could she be so certain he wasn't a man she could love? They got along. He'd found living with her to be surprisingly easy…and pleasurable.

In fact, he might be half in love with her already, but he refused to let himself fall too far. Theirs wouldn't be a grand passion—he'd learned his lesson there—but the kind of love to build a strong marriage upon.

Though his father's talk about marriage had irritated him, at his core, Ben was also a traditional guy.

Marriage made sense. The way he saw it, if he and Poppy could like each other, they could eventually love each other. If they married, they could raise their child together. No joint custody. No weekend visitation.

Of course, that was a lot of ifs. But the possibility intrigued him. When Ben had decided he wanted to make medicine his career and follow in the footsteps of his grandfather and dad, he'd devoted himself to his studies and to the extracurricular activities that looked good on a med school application. He was used to setting objectives and achieving his goals.

All he had to do was follow that same formula. He'd formulate a plan to make Poppy fall in love with him. Failure wasn't an option.

Not with the future happiness of his child at stake.

Chapter Fifteen

In the span of a week, the pendulum of Poppy's relationship with Ben had swung from comfortable to strained back to comfortable. She wasn't quite sure of the reason. At first she'd blamed the strain on the fact she'd told him quite honestly he was a man she would never love.

Even though up to this point Ben had demonstrated he was everything Bill was not, she'd been fooled before. Her ex had seemed to be the man of her dreams…at first.

The fact was, Ben seemed so perfect it scared her. How could she trust her judgment when she'd been so wrong before?

When she'd told Ben she was headed over to Anna's house for a monthly book club meeting on Tuesday, he mentioned Tripp had invited him to come along. This would be Poppy's first time attending the meeting of a close-knit group of friends and she had the feeling Anna had pushed to have her included.

While Poppy was happy she wouldn't have to walk in

alone, having Ben with her felt weird. She knew the women brought spouses and even their children, but Ben wasn't her husband.

What would it be like to have Ben for a husband?

She immediately pushed the thought from her head. Ben was easy to live with, at least so far. She didn't have to walk on eggshells and make sure to give him his space like she'd had to do with Bill. He didn't dominate every conversation with his interests. He seemed genuinely interested in her and her life.

So far, she hadn't seen any warning signs. Women flirted with him. He was friendly, courteous but nothing more. Of course, she'd also seen him glancing at pretty women with a look of appreciation in his eyes.

A yellow flag, but not a red one.

Perhaps she could put her toe in the water and give him more of a chance than she had so far. Not with marriage in mind, but with genuine friendship as a possible goal.

"What do you think of their new place?" Ben asked as they walked up the sidewalk to the new ranch house Tripp and Anna had built on Tripp's parents' land.

It was a large sprawling structure with big windows and a stone façade. Although the landscaping was new, the flowers were in full bloom.

"This is my first time here." Her feet slowed almost imperceptibly as the front steps loomed.

"That surprises me."

"I don't know why." Poppy forced a conversational tone. "I was a good friend of Tripp's first wife, which makes things a bit awkward. Although I do hope Anna and I will end up being friends."

"Is it hard for you to see Tripp with her?"

Poppy swallowed past a sudden lump in her throat. "I miss Gayle so much."

"That doesn't answer the question."

"I accept that life goes on." Poppy puffed out her cheeks

then released the air. "Gayle would want Tripp to be happy. And, while it kills me to admit it, in many ways Anna is better suited to him."

"How so?"

"Both Tripp and Anna love Jackson Hole. Though she'd grown up here, Gayle was a big-city girl. And Anna has a good relationship with his parents. Gayle always said that in-laws were great…as long as they were two thousand miles away."

"Interesting."

"I don't want to give you the wrong impression." Poppy placed a hand on Ben's sleeve. "Gayle and Tripp were very happy. When she died he was devastated."

"That's why it's important never to love too deeply."

Poppy brought her brows together. "What do you mean by that?"

But before he could answer, the door swung open and Anna and Tripp greeted them. While Anna looked elegant as always in a paisley wrap dress and strappy heeled sandals, Tripp had gone über-casual in jeans, chambray shirt and boots.

"I'm taking you with me to the kitchen." Anna took Poppy's arm then shifted her gaze to Ben. "The men will be in the family room. Tripp will get you whatever you want to drink."

"I'm on call tonight," Ben informed her. "Anything non-alcoholic works for me."

To Poppy's surprise, before he turned to go with Tripp, Ben brushed his lips against her cheek. "Later."

Supremely conscious of Anna's speculative gaze, Poppy kept her expression serene even as heat crept up her neck. They were halfway to the kitchen with Anna ready to pounce when the doorbell rang.

"That has to be Betsy and Ryan," Anna said.

While Anna headed to the front door, Poppy continued on to the kitchen. Women were everywhere: standing by the counters talking, sitting at the table. She saw Lexi bent over, pulling a plate of appetizers from the oven.

"Do you need any help?" she asked her coworker.

"Thanks, but I've got it under control." Lexi put the baking pan on a cooling rack, her pretty face flushed from the heat.

Like Anna, Lexi wore a dress, one in hunter green that was a perfect foil for her dark bob and creamy complexion. When Anna had informed Poppy the event was casual, she'd pulled on her last pair of black pants that still fit and coupled it with a bulky cotton sweater in blocks of red, black and white. Her ballet flat shoes were more comfortable than stylish.

Until Betsy entered the room wearing jeans and a simple flowered top, Poppy felt as if she'd been invited to a party and given the wrong dress code. Only when Mary Karen moved to ooh and aah over Betsy's little boy, and Poppy noticed the mother of five was also wearing jeans, did she relax.

"Come over here, Poppy." Mary Karen motioned to her. "I bet it's been a while since you've held a little one. You're going to need to get in some practice. Might as well start now. Love the glasses, by the way."

Poppy didn't feel particularly attractive this evening, but she appreciated the compliment. "Thanks, M.K."

"Nate is almost a year." Betsy kept a firm grip on her wriggling son. "Not all that little anymore."

"He's the smallest one here," Mary Karen pointed out. "He'll have to do."

The dark-haired boy with the big gray eyes went easily into Poppy's arms. But he was surprisingly heavy and after only a few seconds he squirmed to get down. Poppy glanced at Betsy and she nodded.

The second the nine-month-old's sneaker-clad feet hit the floor, he was off and running.

"Isn't he pretty young to be walking?" Poppy asked.

Mary Karen smiled. "I've had a couple walk that early while Sophie waited until thirteen months to take a first step."

"About fifty percent of babies walk by one year. But anywhere from nine to sixteen months is considered normal," Michelle Davis, a pediatrician, added.

The conversation then turned to babies and children. In the past, Poppy would have been bored stiff, but now she was fascinated. Soon, this world would be her reality.

"Food is ready," Lexi announced. In addition to being a wife, mom and a social worker, Lexi also ran a catering business. While each woman attending the book club contributed to the dinner, Lexi always brought the entrée. She turned to Poppy. "Could you please let the men and kids know it's time to come and fill their plates?"

Poppy couldn't figure out why Lexi had asked her, until she realized that Anna was busy setting out the napkins and plates.

She'd passed the family room on the way back to the kitchen, but had only glanced at it. As Poppy stopped in the entryway, she took a moment to study the room. The ceilings were high with open beams and the massive furniture was deep burgundy leather. The floors were hardwood with woven rugs.

There was a large flat screen on one wall that was tuned to some sporting channel. Kids of all ages, shapes and sizes littered the room. Several older girls were putting a puzzle together on the coffee table. Poppy recognized one of them as Lexi's oldest, Addie.

"The food is ready," Poppy announced. "Lexi said to come and get it."

Two identical blond-haired boys jumped to their feet. But Travis put a hand on their shoulders. "Ladies first," he told his sons.

The girls smirked as they sauntered past.

Ben rose from the sofa where he'd been talking to Travis and moseyed over to her side. With a finger, he pushed a strand of hair back from her face. "How's it going?"

The concern in his eyes told her she hadn't been entirely successful in hiding her earlier trepidation. The fact he'd not only noticed, but cared, warmed her heart. "I was worried I'd dressed too casually, but I'm fine."

His gaze dropped and he slowly surveyed her from top to bottom. She could feel the heat beneath her clothes rising to the surface wherever his gaze touched. "You look more than fine to me."

An invisible web of attraction formed around them. Poppy found herself leaning into him.

"Hey, break it up." Tripp punched Ben in the shoulder as he walked past. "This is a G-rated cvent."

"Get your eyes checked, Randall," Ben said mildly. "We're just talking."

"I know what both of you are thinking," Tripp said to him, then shifted his gaze to Poppy.

Poppy just laughed. "You need to tout your talent as a mind reader during your upcoming mayoral bid. Trust me, it'll set you apart."

"Thanks for the suggestion." There was a speculative gleam in Tripp's eyes as Ben took her arm.

With his dark gray pants and pewter-colored shirt, Ben fit right in with the men whose attire ranged from Tripp's jeans to Nick Delacourt, who'd come directly from a business meeting in his suit.

As she mulled over the clothing, she decided she really was a stick-in-the-mud. What happened to her spontaneity? Really, how many people spent time analyzing what everyone was wearing instead of simply focusing on enjoying themselves?

No more, Poppy told herself. Tonight she would have a good time. She would enjoy Ben's company and participate in the book club discussion. And she wouldn't give one more thought to clothing, glasses, or whether the women liked her enough to ask her back again.

Food was spread out on a large granite breakfast bar. With a serious expression, she pointed out to Ben that he was setting a bad example for the children by avoiding the salad because it included olives. A smile of pleasure lit his eyes at her teasing tone.

When he rested his hand lightly on her shoulder, she had to admit the contact felt good. But once all the men had gotten their food, Anna shooed them and the children out of the kitchen, promising them dessert later.

Poppy had expected the women to start on the book discussion while they ate. Instead the talk turned personal as they sat around the large oval table with plates of food before them.

"Travis said Keenan might be out of prison before Christmas," Mary Karen said then sighed in ecstasy when her lips closed around a bite of the mango chicken piccata, the entrée Lexi had brought.

"This is fabulous." Betsy cast an approving glance in Lexi's direction before shifting her focus back to Mary Karen. "Travis heard correctly. The release may even be as early as this fall."

"I can't imagine being imprisoned for something I didn't do." Poppy's heart twisted at the thought of what Keenan must have endured. "He has to be so angry."

"Not as much as you'd think." Betsy's eyes softened. "He'd done a lot of growing up before he went to prison. I think he's even more mature now."

"I'm happy for him." Lexi reached across the table and squeezed Betsy's hand.

"Thanks." Betsy's smile lit her whole face. "But I'm not the only one with good news. Poppy and Ben have some, too."

"I'm not sure an unplanned pregnancy actually qualifies as good news," Poppy said, then immediately felt as if she'd been disloyal to the baby. "Although a new life is always something to celebrate."

"There are a few of us who've been in your situation." Mary Karen chuckled. "In fact we could probably form our own club."

Laughter rippled around the table.

"It looks as if you and Ben are getting along well," Anna said.

"He's moved in with her," Lexi informed the others.

Michelle looked surprised. "Really?"

Don't be shy, Poppy told herself. Like Mary Karen had said, no one here would judge her. "It seemed a good next step."

"But why your apartment?" Michelle asked.

"I don't want to tell you." Poppy dropped her gaze to her hands. "You'll think it's silly."

"No, we won't," the women protested almost in one breath.

She wouldn't tell them it was a power thing, that she worried moving in with Ben would make her feel as if he had all the power. Even if they wouldn't judge her, and might even understand, it was too personal.

Instead she gave them a reason that was close to the truth. "When I discovered I was pregnant, my life turned upside down. I've had a lot of change in my life this past year. I'd moved back to Jackson Hole, got a new job and a new place to live. I honestly couldn't bear the thought of one more change."

It was true…as far as it went.

"That was nice of Ben to understand," Anna said in that soft, thoughtful way of hers.

The other women nodded.

"He's a nice guy." Poppy found herself surprised by the fact that the words rang true.

"Do you think you'll get married?" Michelle asked.

"Our first priority is getting to know each other even better."

"That's what David and I decided to do." July Wahl, whose husband was an E.R. doctor, spoke for the first time.

"You were pregnant when you got married?" Poppy asked cautiously.

Mary Karen gave a hoot of laughter. "Nothing quite that mundane."

Lexi smiled and took a sip of her wine.

Anna added a thumbnail size of pasta salad to her plate.

"David and I had a one-night stand when he was in Chicago attending a conference and I was working as a photographer for the paper." July sensed she had Poppy's full attention and grinned. "Through some strange quirk of fate, I took a job photographing national parks and went into early labor while I was doing the Yellowstone shoot. Guess who was the doctor on duty when I showed up at the E.R.?"

Poppy widened her eyes. "This sounds like a soap opera."

July laughed and took a sip of wine. "We took time to get to know each other, got married and now have two wonderful little boys."

"If you think about the reason that soaps are so popular, it's because in many ways they mirror real life," Lexi said with a wicked grin. "At least they do if you look at this group."

"Of everyone here tonight I think Anna, Michelle and I are the only ones who didn't have a bun in the oven before we walked down the aisle," Betsy said.

Anna cocked her head. "I believe you're right."

"You and Tripp better get right on that," Mary Karen said in that same no-nonsense tone Poppy had heard her use with her kids.

"We're working on it." The Madonna-like smile that graced Anna's pretty face told Poppy news of a pregnancy would soon be forthcoming.

"Forget about the book discussion," July said. "Let's just talk sex."

"Poppy's face is turning red," Mary Karen said as she chortled.

"If you keep that up, M.K., she's not going to want to come again," Lexi warned.

Poppy laughed, but wanted to tell Lexi and all the others that this was the most fun she'd had since she'd returned to Jackson Hole.

Was it because she knew these women didn't judge her? Or was it her decision to not be so uptight, to not worry so much about the future implications of everything. To simply let go and enjoy?

"I liked the book," Anna said. "Though we're already halfway through the year, I like the idea of choosing a word to be my focus for the year."

Anna went on to explain that the nonfiction book was recommended to her by one of her patients. She'd picked it up at the local bookstore and found it to be a quick, but inspiring read.

"I also enjoyed it," Betsy admitted. "Though I'm still not sure what word I'll choose."

"It's a big decision," Anna told her.

"I think it'd be good for me," Mary Karen said. "With five kids and a husband with a busy medical practice, I sometimes feel like I catch myself coming and going. Though I'm not big on introspection, I believe a focus would be good for me and for my family."

"I agree," Poppy found herself saying. "There have been so many changes in my life during this past year it's easy to feel overwhelmed. I'd like a word that would keep me focused on what's important."

"Do you have one in mind?" Lexi asked her.

"Not yet." Poppy stabbed a green bean. "But I have the feeling I'll know it when I see it."

Chapter Sixteen

After some spirited discussion—and just before they were ready to call it a night—Poppy was hit with inspiration.

"Freedom," she told the others. "That's my word."

"Freedom," Lexi repeated, a thoughtful look on her face.

"It feels right," Poppy told the women.

"We should set aside a time at each book club meeting to talk about our words." Mary Karen rose from the table to help load the dishwasher. "Since there were so many who couldn't attend tonight, we need to make sure the others know we're doing this so they have a chance to participate."

"Good thinking, Mary Karen." Anna nodded her approval. "Perhaps we should divide up the names. That way we can make sure everyone is contacted."

Mary Karen nodded, brought a finger to her lips. "Let's see, who do we have—"

"I'll call Rachel," Michelle said, referring to a friend who lived part of the year in Jackson Hole and the rest in California.

"Poppy, you get Mitzi. I'm sure you'll see her since she practices with Ben. I'll give you Kate Dennes, too, since she's Mitzi's best friend."

Poppy wasn't sure what surprised her more, that they were having her call people when she wasn't even part of the group, or that Mitzi was a member.

"I don't mind helping out," Poppy began slowly after Mary Karen had barked out a few more assignments then paused for breath. "But wouldn't it be better to have someone who was actually part of the group call them?"

Mary Karen tilted her blond head and looked at Poppy as if she'd spoken in a language she didn't understand. "You're part of this group."

Now Poppy was confused. "I'm just filling in tonight."

"Don't you want to be part of the group?" Anna's brows pulled together in puzzlement.

"I thought you had fun." Hurt filled Lexi's eyes.

"I did have fun. And I want to be part of the group." Poppy took a deep breath. "I didn't think you wanted me to be a regular member."

"We invited you. You came. You're a regular now." July's tone might be brusque but the softness in her eyes told Poppy she understood. "We're all happy about that."

Everyone around the table nodded.

Pleasure slid through Poppy's veins like warm honey. It had been a long time since she'd experienced this sense of belonging. "I'll be happy to contact Mitzi and Kate."

"Now that we've got that settled, can we have dessert?" Mary Karen's tone stopped just short of a whine.

"I know the last time we met we agreed to try healthy dessert options," July began. "I was fully prepared to bring something low-cal until I ran across a new red velvet cake recipe. I made it for David and the boys last week and OMG, it is so fabulous."

"I would have to kill you, dear sister-in-law, if you

brought a low-cal treat," Mary Karen said, her tone only half joking. "I've been dying for something sweet all day."

"So have I," Betsy admitted. "I even took Nate and Puffy for an extra long walk today so I could have dessert without feeling guilty."

She grinned. "Never let it be said July Wahl disappoints."

A cheer rose up. Poppy found herself joining in.

"I'll call in the hoard from the hinterlands." Anna grinned. "*After* we've gotten our piece of cake."

"I like the way this woman thinks." Mary Karen shot Poppy a wink.

Once the women's plates and coffee cups were full, Anna informed the men and children dessert was served. With the announcement, the segregation ended. Those with children stayed in the kitchen where the floors could easily absorb the mess. Those without—or who'd left their children at home—wandered into the living room.

"David's parents love watching the boys." July settled herself into a chair wide enough for two, and patted the spot next to her.

"We haven't gone out much lately, so they were eager to watch them." David dropped down next to July and slipped his arm around her shoulders. The movement was so smooth it seemed second nature.

David had been handsome as a young man but, like Ben, he was one of those guys who only improved with time.

"It's nice to finally be able to hear myself think." Tripp slipped an arm around his wife's waist. "Travis's boys are Xbox crazy."

"Which is good because it keeps them occupied," Anna said lightly. "They're very high energy."

"Are you going to find out what you're having?" July asked Poppy, licking the cream cheese frosting off her fork.

Poppy had taken a seat on the sofa with Ben. She glanced at him. "We're leaning that way."

Ben squeezed her hand and smiled.

The conversation shifted to the upcoming Taste of Jackson Hole event then to a projected golf course development that Winn Ferris was attempting to get approved.

"Poppy, didn't you and Winn date for a while?" Anna tilted her head. "Or am I thinking of someone else?"

"Who hasn't that guy gone after?" Tripp said with a scowl. He glanced at his wife and his expression softened. "For a while he had you in his crosshairs."

Anna patted her husband's shoulder. "You were the only man I ever wanted."

Poppy sensed Ben's gaze on her.

"Winn and I had dinner a couple of times." Poppy kept her tone offhand. "Friends. No big deal."

"Not like Ben," July teased. "He swept you off your feet."

"I convinced Poppy she couldn't live without me." Ben's tone might be light but the eyes that he'd fixed on her were intense.

Poppy smiled then impulsively leaned over and rested a hand against his cheek. "Unlike Winn, you were impossible to resist."

At the flash of heat in Ben's eyes, her body began to hum. By the time the evening concluded and they were on their way home the hum had turned into an electrical charge strong enough to power the town of Jackson. The air in the car snapped and sizzled.

As they climbed the steps to her second-story apartment, Ben took Poppy's arm, steadying her. They paused at the door while he took out his key.

"They want me to be a permanent member of the group." Poppy knew it was silly, but she couldn't quite keep the pleasure from her voice.

"Of course they do." He pushed the door open and stepped aside to let her enter.

Poppy sauntered past him then dropped her bag to the floor. "I thought I was simply filling in."

Ben liked seeing light dance in her eyes. Liked knowing

the other women had made her feel welcome. He took a seat next to her on the sofa. Not too close. But close enough if the vibes he'd picked up on the way home were accurate, he wouldn't be far when the firestorm hit.

"I'm sorry. I've been blathering on." She looked chagrined. "I haven't even asked what you thought of the evening."

"I enjoyed it." Ben realized he'd never felt fully part of the community until tonight. "I wouldn't mind going back."

"The book club meets every month," Poppy began. "Spouses are always wel—"

She stopped herself. A flush of red traveled up her neck to color her cheeks. "And significant others, er, boyfriends, ah—"

Ben could see she was floundering, sensed her distress and found it quite charming.

"—and guys like you."

It took everything he had to keep his lips from twitching. He lifted a brow. "Guys like me?"

She gave an embarrassed laugh. "I'm not sure how else to say it. You have to admit we have a unique relationship."

"One I like very much." He traced a finger down her arm. "I enjoyed going to the party with you and knowing we'd be coming home together when the evening ended."

"I liked that part, too," she said.

"Kind of like being married." Ben laced his fingers with hers. "I think it'd be nice having someone you care about around at the end of the day."

Poppy's gaze dropped to her entwined hands. "Bill was gone more than he was home. I told myself I didn't mind. I thought I'd get used to being alone. I never did."

"Your experience taught you what you want," he pointed out. "And what you don't want in a relationship. That's huge."

With the warmth of his hands on hers, Poppy realized Ben was right. And she realized something even more important. The man sitting beside her was himself, not a clone of Bill.

Freedom.

What did the word she'd chosen tonight mean to her? It meant the freedom to make her own choices, to choose her own path. To be free of old attitudes and more importantly, freedom from irrational fears. Freedom to be spontaneous.

"I want—" Poppy swallowed hard then traced Ben's lips with her fingers "—you."

He slid even closer and pulled her tight. "You have me."

"It's not like I can get pregnant or anything," she said in a lighthearted tone that brought a smile to his face.

"One less worry." He carefully removed her glasses and placed them on the end table before his mouth lowered to nuzzle her neck.

"No worries tonight," she said in a schoolmarm tone. "Not allowed."

He nibbled her ear, sending pleasure shooting through her body. "Is this allowed?"

"Most certainly," she said in a voice that sounded breathless.

"How about this?" His lips moved to her mouth. By the time the kiss ended, Poppy had difficulty recalling the question.

She tried—unsuccessfully—to slow her breathing. "Wow."

His smile widened into a grin. "I'll consider that a yes."

"You're looking pretty smug."

"Just gathering up my courage."

She cocked her head.

His fingers slipped under her sweater, his hands cool against her burning skin. "Venturing into unknown territory."

"I believe you explored that area, and quite thoroughly as I recall not all that—" She gasped when those searching fingers found the lacy edge of her bra.

"I take that as another yes." With quick, experienced fingers he unfastened the scrap of fabric to bare her skin to his gaze. The tips of her nipples hardened beneath his fingers.

She arched back. "Please," came out on a strangled cry of pleasure.

Ben pushed her sweater up all the way and replaced his fingers with his mouth. When he began to suck, heat shot straight to her core.

"Let me help you," he said when her frantic hands tugged at the sweater.

In seconds her pants and underwear soon followed the sweater on the floor.

"Now you're the one overdressed," she panted.

"Easily remedied." In seconds his clothes joined hers.

His hands slid up and down her body, his mouth following, plundering and teasing.

"Beautiful," Ben murmured, his hand skimming the slight round of her belly before dipping lower and cupping her.

Poppy bucked. Her body shuddered. "I want you inside me."

"Thanks for the invitation."

She gave a snorting laugh that caught in her throat when he slowly slid inside, his arms tensed on either side of her.

"Hard," she ordered, writhing beneath him.

"I thought I should be gentle."

"Think again." She wrapped her legs around him.

It was tricky. The sofa was, after all, only so wide. But she wouldn't—couldn't—take time to move to the floor or a bed. Poppy's hips moved like pistons as he pushed in and out, his breath coming in pants, matching hers.

She tried to hold on, but the need for him swamped her. She quivered and clenched, crying out his name as the orgasm hit.

Seconds later he gave one final thrust and filled her, then collapsed on top of her, skin wet with sweat.

"That was the best dessert," she said with shaky laughter. "Even better than the red velvet cake."

Ben chuckled softly as he nuzzled her neck. He remained inside her, and before long, he was hard again. The fullness had her body thrumming with anticipating. With her arms wrapped around his neck she began to move beneath him.

Ben looked up, met her gaze. "Don't tell me—"

She kissed him hard. "Yep, I want seconds."

Chapter Seventeen

The next morning Ben woke before the alarm. He took a moment to study the woman sleeping beside him. Poppy's dark hair was tousled around her face and she'd flung one arm across her eyes, as if the soft light filtering through the window shades was too bright.

Last night he'd pulled out one of his white T-shirts when she'd insisted she couldn't sleep naked. It had ridden up while she slept and barely covered those full, luscious breasts. She looked…beautiful.

Mine, he thought. *All mine.*

Giving in to temptation, he brushed a light kiss across her cheek.

Stirring, her eyes fluttered open. Then her lips lifted. "Hi."

"Good morning."

"I'd ask if you were interested in staying in bed a little longer but you have that 'I need to get going,' look on your face." She covered a yawn with her fingers.

"A hip replacement is calling my name." He gave in to temptation and kissed her again. "I'd much rather stay here with you."

Poppy sighed when he pulled back. "Will you be home for dinner tonight?"

"I won't," he said with honest regret. "Basketball at the Y."

Poppy propped herself up on one elbow. "Are you planning to eat prior to the game?"

"I doubt I'll have time."

"What if I have a snack to tide me over, then whenever you get home we can eat together?"

Just the fact that she would offer made Ben realize how far they'd come. "Great plan."

"I'm always thinking." She slipped her shirt over her head in one swift movement.

Desire hit him like a bone mallet. Ben glanced at the clock. Could he make it work?

Poppy wound her arms around his neck, her taut nipples brushing against his bare chest.

She gazed at him through lowered lashes. "Someone once told me we make time for what's important."

To hell with it, Ben thought and crushed his mouth against hers.

If Poppy had known she'd be stopping by Ben's office today, she'd have worn a suit rather than a dress to work. Most of those in his office were strangers to her, and there was always the possibility she'd run into his father.

Only a couple hours ago, Poppy had been asked by a county judge to schedule a meeting with Dr. Sanchez. Mitzi had been the specialist who'd repaired a fractured hand on a little girl in Poppy's caseload.

The child's family doctor was concerned over the girl's therapy progress. The judge was reconsidering his decision to allow the eight-year-old to remain in a home where the mother had previously been cited for neglect.

Poppy called the orthopedic clinic shortly after receiving the request. To her surprise, Ben's associate had squeezed her in over the lunch hour. Not wanting to keep Mitzi waiting, Poppy arrived ten minutes early.

Professionally decorated in shades of gray and burgundy, the clinic waiting room had an aura of understated wealth and comfort. There was an area off to one side that appeared to be for younger patients, filled with books, puzzles, a wooden train on a table and a television tuned to a kids' channel.

A receptionist sat inputting data into the computer behind an opened glass window. She looked up when Poppy's heels clattered on the tile floor.

"I'm sorry," the woman said in a pleasant, well-modulated tone even before Poppy reached the window. "The office is closed between twelve and one."

"I have an appointment with Dr. Sanchez at twelve-fifteen." Poppy flashed a smile. "Could you please tell her Poppy Westover is here?"

"One moment." The redhead lifted the receiver just as Ben's father came through the door.

He came to an abrupt stop. Surprise skittered across his face. "Poppy. Hello. Unfortunately, if you're here to see Ben, he's in surgery."

"Actually I'm here to meet with Mitzi, er, Dr. Sanchez, about a case."

The older man smiled. "That's right. You're a social worker."

"Ms. Westover, Dr. Sanchez isn't quite ready." The receptionist gestured to the waiting room. "If you'll take a seat, I'll let you know as soon as she's available."

"Helene, tell Dr. Sanchez to come to my office when she's free," Ben's father said. "Poppy will be with me.

"Dori and I were sorry to miss the party on Saturday,"

John said easily as he ushered her down the hall. "We wished we could have spent time with you and Ben."

"Ben mentioned something about an anniversary party?"

"Our friends were celebrating forty years of marriage. Dori had been one of the bridesmaids." He opened a door at the end of the hall and motioned her inside. "I'm glad our paths crossed. There's something I need to clear up."

He must have caught her look of panic because he smiled and winked. "Trust me. This won't hurt a bit."

The smile was so like Ben's that Poppy felt herself relax. Still, her heart fluttered as she stepped into the large, well-appointed office. Diplomas and various certificates hung on the wall along with a Robert Wood painting of the Grand Tetons. A magnificent desk in glossy cherrywood dominated the room, along with a monitor twice the size of the one in Poppy's office.

At his direction, Poppy took a seat and discovered the barrel chairs in burgundy leather were not only stylish but comfortable.

"I believe my son told you about our discussion concerning his responsibility to you." He folded his large hands, suddenly serious. "I admire you for being willing to take on the challenge of raising a child alone, but there's no reason you should have to face this by yourself."

"I'm not." Poppy leaned forward. "Ben is more than shouldering his share of the responsibility."

"He hasn't married you."

"I wouldn't marry him even if he asked."

"You—what?" The man blinked. "What's wrong with my son?"

"Nothing," Poppy assured him. "It's just that I was married before. To a man who lied and cheated on me. It was a horrible experience and one I don't care to repeat."

"Then don't."

Poppy felt herself relax. "Thank you for understanding."

"You shouldn't marry a man who'd cheat and lie to you.

But Ben isn't like your ex-husband. He's decent and honorable. A good man and someone you can trust."

"I hope I'm not interrupting—" Mitzi stood in the partially open doorway, looking exceptionally pretty in a bold dress of lime green and fuchsia. Her white lab coat served as a nice buffer to the eye-popping colors.

Relieved, Poppy jumped to her feet. "No, John, er, Dr. Campbell, was kind enough to keep me company."

She turned back to Ben's father and extended her hand. "Good speaking with you."

The doctor took Poppy's hand then covered it with his other one. "Promise you'll come out to the ranch again soon."

"I will." Poppy turned to Mitzi. "Thanks for agreeing to meet with me on such short notice."

Poppy followed Mitzi to her office, noticing the doctor's four-inch heels were the same shade of green as her dress.

"Happy to help." Mitzi gestured to a pair of chairs. "Have a seat."

Poppy eyed the two wingbacks and decided on the bright blue leather one. "I love primary colors. But then I gravitate to the bold."

"So do I." Instead of moving behind the desk, Mitzi sat in the adjacent chair in cherry red. "How's it working out?"

"I have the particulars of Amanda Burlinsky's situation right here." Poppy reached into the black eel-skin briefcase and pulled out the papers.

"I wasn't referring to Mandy." Mitzi's lips lifted in amusement. "Though I definitely want to discuss her situation. I was referring to you and Ben living together."

Poppy's fingers tightened on the papers. "It's going well. We went to the book club meeting at Tripp and Anna Randall's last night."

She quickly explained about choosing a word and Mitzi promised to explain it all to Kate.

"Ben went with you?" Mitzi asked.

"Lots of men were there."

"I know, but I'd asked him several times while we were dating if he wanted to go with me and he always had some excuse." Mitzi's gaze grew thoughtful. "And you said living together is going well?"

Poppy nodded.

"That surprises me." Mitzi's expression turned pensive. "I'd have sworn he'd be difficult to live with."

"Why?"

Though they were alone, Mitzi's tone lowered to a confidential whisper. "It's just we both know Ben likes things his own way."

Poppy didn't have to fake confusion. His colleague could have been describing Poppy's ex, but not the man who currently had his clothes stowed in the guest bedroom of her apartment.

Unless...

A cold chill traveled up Poppy's spine. Unless she hadn't been paying attention. Unless once again she'd missed critical signs. Her heart slammed against her ribs. "I haven't noticed that from him, but then it's early days yet."

"Perhaps it was just our dynamics." Mitzi's tone said that was extremely doubtful. "I'm happy it's working out for you."

"Like I said, it's early days."

"His parents weren't keen on us being together," Mitzi continued. "Which made it awkward, considering his father is at the helm of this group."

When Poppy didn't respond, Mitzi's sharp-eyed gaze searched her face. "You don't know me or whether I can be trusted. But I can and I'm here for you."

"Okay," was all Poppy could think to say in response.

Mitzi glanced at the file on her lap. "Tell me what's going on with Mandy."

Poppy quickly detailed the situation, sticking to relevant

data. "Basically, the concern is that the mother has been neglectful in not helping her daughter with the therapy."

"The notes I received from Meg Lassiter indicated both the mother and the daughter understood the importance of the exercises and had demonstrated proper technique." Mitzi frowned. "I'm surprised Dr. Pardee didn't call me directly about this instead of contacting the judge."

"I was surprised, too," Poppy told her. "I'd done a home visit and noticed Mandy wasn't using her right hand."

"I'd like to examine her," Mitzi said. "Why don't you bring her and her mother to the office? Have Meg come, too, if she's available."

"I'll set it up." Poppy pulled to her feet. "Thanks, Mitzi."

"I hope things work out between you and Ben," Mitzi said, walking with her to the door.

"Thank you." Poppy saw no need to tell Mitzi that the only thing she wanted was for Ben to be a good father to their baby. If that happened, she'd be satisfied.

Shortly after she arrived home from the office, Poppy opened the refrigerator door and tried to think of a nutritious snack to tide her over until dinner.

She was still staring into the cool depths when she heard the key in the lock. She turned and let the door fall shut. *Ben.*

He smiled and when he started toward her, Poppy's heart flip-flopped.

"I've been looking forward to this all day." He leaned over and kissed her.

With a movement that was beginning to feel natural, Poppy wrapped her arms around his neck and kissed him back. "This is a nice surprise. What happened to the basketball game?"

"Rescheduled." His fingers played with her hair. "They forgot to mention they were resurfacing the floors."

"That's too bad."

"I suppose." Ben's gaze met hers. "After my last surgery, I stopped by the clinic. My dad told me you'd been by—"

"I stopped to discuss a case with Mitzi," Poppy clarified. "She wasn't ready for me when I arrived, so your father and I had some time alone. We, ah, cleared the air."

"He appreciated your honesty," was all Ben said before changing the subject. "What sounds good for dinner?"

"I'm craving spaghetti." Poppy sighed. "But there's no pasta in the house."

"Then let's go get some." He flashed a smile. "It'll be an adventure."

"If you say so." She grabbed her jacket and purse on the way out the door.

"I rarely go to the grocery store." Ben stepped back and opened the car door for her. "I make a list and Angela does the shopping. I believe she enjoys it."

Poppy decided she and Angela would get along. After all, she enjoyed shopping, too.

The grocery store parking lot held only a few cars and trucks. Ben found a space near the door.

An older man who was walking out when they were walking in, slowed his steps and smiled. "Dr. Campbell, good to see you."

"Hello, Lionel. You're looking good."

"Thanks to you," the balding man with the ruddy complexion replied.

"Who's that?" Poppy asked as the man headed for his vehicle.

"Lionel Freeman." Ben kept his tone equally low. "He got a new hip six months ago."

"It can be intoxicating." Poppy thought of Bill and how he'd reveled in the adoration of his patients. "Having people so grateful."

"I don't know about intoxicating." Ben chuckled. "Let's just say it's always better to have a patient happy rather than dissatisfied."

Once they got inside Ben insisted on pushing the cart. The lights overhead were blinding white and the tile floor beneath their feet gleamed.

Ben picked up a cantaloupe. "How do we know if this is a good one?"

"First, look at the color," Poppy said. "The lighter the better. You want it beige, not green. Then push on the blossom end. It should have a nice give, but not too much. And lastly—" she lifted it to her nose and then offered it to him "—you want a sweet smell. But not smelly."

Ben obligingly took a sniff, then glanced at her. "A good one."

"Definitely."

It didn't take long to get checked out but by the time Poppy had pulled out her money, Ben had already swiped his card. The innocent look on his face didn't fool her in the least.

As he pushed the cart to the car, she shot him a warning glance. "I've got a tally going. We're splitting everything fifty-fifty."

"Then tell me what I owe for my share of the rent."

"You don't owe anything."

"You said we were splitting everything."

"You may be living with me, but you're still making house payments." Poppy reached for a sack.

Ben gently, but firmly pushed back her hands. "These are too heavy for you."

"Oh, come on." She fisted her hands on her hips. "I've been doing my own grocery shopping for years."

"You're pregnant," he pointed out. "I'm in charge of lifting sacks. You're in charge of picking perfect produce."

"Okay," she said somewhat sulkily, but had to admit she enjoyed watching him bend over and place the bags in the trunk.

"Better get in the car," he told her as thunder rumbled

ominously in the distance. "Unless you're in the mood for a shower."

It wasn't until her apartment building was in sight that scattered drops of rain began to dot the windshield. Poppy was greeted by a loud clap of thunder when she opened her car door.

"You head inside." Ben glanced up. Dark clouds now blanketed the sky. "I'll take care of the bags."

"I'll unlock the door." Poppy hurried up the steps. Only when she'd reached the door did she realize she'd left her purse in the car. On the way down to retrieve it, she met Ben coming up. At his questioning look, she rolled her eyes. "I left my purse in the car."

"I can get it."

She glanced pointedly at the sacks in his arms. "I'd say you already have your hands full."

After retrieving her bag from the front seat, Poppy moseyed around to the open trunk. She tentatively hefted a sack of toiletries. It had to weigh less than her purse. She chewed on her lower lip and considered the remaining sack. It, too, was only half-filled. If she took these bags up with her, they'd be done.

Another smattering of raindrops made the decision easy. Slinging her purse over her shoulder, Poppy grabbed the handles of the two sacks and headed for the stairs. Several more windblown raindrops hitting her cheeks had her picking up the pace.

She'd almost reached the top of the steps when her foot came down on something. Poppy fought to regain her balance but the sacks in her hands and her heeled sandals made that impossible.

Before she could cry out, she was falling.

Chapter Eighteen

Ben had just placed the sacks on the table when he heard Poppy cry out. He took off running. When he spotted her crumpled body at the bottom of the steps, his heart stopped. In seconds he was at her side.

Tears streamed down her cheeks as she rocked back and forth, hands on her ankle.

"Poppy." He knelt down beside her, ignoring the rain. "Sweetheart, what happened?"

"There was something on the stairs." She sniffled. "I fell."

"You took quite a tumble," he agreed, keeping his tone calm. "What hurts?"

"My ankle." She swiped at her tears with the back of her hand then a look of absolute terror filled her eyes. "Do you think I hurt the baby?"

His heart, which had resumed beating, stopped again. Still, he'd had years of keeping his feelings hidden from anxious patients. "The baby is fine. He or she is well protected by the fluid in the amniotic sac. Now, I'm going to do a quick exam to make sure it's okay to move you."

It didn't take long to ascertain that while she'd probably be sore all over tomorrow, it was her ankle that was the problem. There was slight joint instability and swelling had already begun.

"You'll be fine," he said in a voice that shook slightly. He didn't think she had a clue just how badly she could have been hurt. "Let's get you inside and put some ice on that ankle."

He made quick work of clearing the steps of food and toiletries then scooped Poppy into his arms. Ignoring her protests that she could walk with just a little help, he carried her up the stairs and into the apartment.

After she was settled in a chair, he quickly wrapped her ankle before lifting her leg to the coffee table and placing it on a pillow he'd confiscated from the bedroom. "Ice bag?"

"I have one of those gel things in the freezer."

He retrieved it then gently molded it around the puffy ankle.

"Are you sure it's not broken?"

He gave her a look and she felt somewhat sheepish. "Of course you're sure."

"We may need to x-ray it tomorrow," he said. "But it appears to be a partial tearing of the ligament."

"Oh, well, if that's all—" she quipped, then winced as she tried to reposition herself.

Thunder crackled overhead, rattling the windows.

"Ben," she said. "You have to get the food."

"To hell with the food."

"Please." Her voice turned pleading. "Just run down and pick up the stuff before the rain really gets started. I'll be fine."

He couldn't believe she could get so upset over a hundred dollars' worth of food. But she was, so after making sure the ice bag was firmly in place, he did as she asked.

By the time he brought up the last two bags, the rain had turned into a downpour. Because he knew Poppy wouldn't relax until the food needing to be refrigerated had been put away, he made quick work of that process.

He'd just placed a carton of ice cream in the freezer when, out of the corner of his eye, he saw her attempting to stand.

He hurried to her side. "What are you doing?"

"I want to go to the bathroom," she said blinking back tears. "I want to be sure..." She took a deep breath and released it. "I want to check if there's any bleeding. I know you said the baby is cushioned but I'm worried."

"Let me help you." Carefully removing the ice bag, he saw the look of surprise in her eyes when he picked her up. "No need to argue. This one you won't win."

She didn't say a word, merely rested her head against his shoulder. He felt her tremble and inwardly cursed those blasted steps. They weren't safe. Not for a pregnant woman.

When he sat her down but made no move to leave, she gave him a nudge. "I'll be all right alone. Just give me a few minutes."

"I'll be outside the door."

Though it had to have been only a minute or two, Ben was ready to walk in when she called for him. He opened the door. The first thing he saw was the relief on her face.

"No blood," she told him before he could ask.

He exhaled the breath he didn't realize he'd been holding. "I told you the baby was okay."

She held out a hand to him and he lifted her into his arms. "Do you feel better now?"

"A little. I mean, no bleeding is a good sign." The lines of worry had returned to her brow. "But perhaps I should still call Travis. I realize you're a doctor and all, but broken bones are your specialty, not babies."

"If it'd make you feel better, we can call him." Ben laid

her gently back on the sofa and placed the ice bag back on her ankle.

"Is it too late to call?"

Ben pulled his cell phone from his pocket. "It's not even eight."

Even if it had been the middle of the night, Ben wouldn't have hesitated. Bothering Travis was worth easing Poppy's mind. And his, as well, he realized.

Travis answered immediately. Cutting the social niceties short, Ben explained the situation.

"Considering there's no bleeding, I'm confident there's no problem," Travis told him. "But if you'd like, I can come by and confirm we still have a good strong heartbeat."

"I'd appreciate it," Ben said. "Let me give you Poppy's address."

When the call disconnected, he turned to Poppy. "He'll be right over."

"I hope he doesn't think I'm a big baby." Two bright swaths of pink stained her cheeks. "I mean, I could have waited and gone in tomorrow."

"You could have," he admitted, taking a seat beside her. "But you'll sleep better tonight after you get the all clear from Travis."

"You probably think I'm being silly," she said, her voice shaking.

"Then I'm silly, too." He slipped an arm around her shoulders. "Even though I'm ninety-nine point nine percent certain that we have absolutely nothing to worry about, I'd feel better having it confirmed."

"You really do want this baby," Poppy said, her voice filled with wonder.

"Did you think I didn't?"

"I didn't know for sure."

"That's what this is all about," he said, gesturing to the small living room. "Getting to know each other."

"Yes," she said. "That's what living under the same roof is all about."

"But after what happened tonight, some changes need to be made."

Poppy stilled. "What kind of changes?"

"We're moving to my house." His tone brooked no argument. "And we'll be doing that tonight."

Travis arrived fewer than ten minutes after Ben's call. Apparently he and Mary Karen had taken the boys out for pizza and were just down the street. When he told her the baby's heartbeat was loud and strong, she grasped Ben's hand and began to cry.

It was as if a huge weight had slipped from her shoulders. When Ben had started packing up essentials, she didn't protest.

His argument that the stairs to her apartment posed a continuing danger couldn't be refuted. She knew as the pregnancy progressed and her center of gravity shifted, the risk of falling would only increase.

Next time I might not be so lucky.

She automatically lowered her hand to rest on the little mound. Nothing was more important than her child. And somehow, the thought of living in Ben's house no longer filled her with the same panic it would have only a few weeks earlier.

Somewhere along the way, she'd begun to trust Ben. He'd certainly proven how much he cared for her and their child tonight.

"Poppy?"

She shifted her gaze to the doorway. He set her suitcase on the floor of his guest room, where he'd carried her when they'd first arrived.

"I'd be happy to help you unpack. Or Angela can do it tomorrow, if you'd prefer. Right now, I don't want you up on that ankle any more than necessary."

"Thank you."

A look of surprise skittered across his face. "For what?"

She held out her hands to him and he crossed the room to sit beside her on the bed. "For not yelling at me for climbing the stairs."

"You've gone up and down those stairs with groceries more times than you can probably count," he said. "There's no way you could have known a child would leave an eraser on one of the steps."

"I'm not the type to take chances."

His gaze settled on her for a heartbeat. Then two. "I'm not, either."

"We're not talking about me climbing the stairs anymore," she said after a long pause.

He shook his head. "We're not."

Ben thought about Kristin, remembered how he'd felt when she'd walked away. He'd taken a chance with her and it hadn't turned out. While he wasn't ready to give his whole heart to Poppy, he had to admit that she'd already corralled a good part of it. More than he'd ever thought he'd be willing to give up.

"I'd like to try," she said.

"I would, too."

"I don't want to be in this bedroom." She met his gaze. "I want to be in your room. With you. If you want me there, that is."

He stroked her cheek and smiled. "I already cleared out part of the closet."

The next weeks were the happiest of Ben's life. Poppy had opened her heart and he'd made himself at home there. They went to church, had breakfast with friends and, once her sprained ankle was fully healed, they'd gone on a long nature walk on his parents' ranch.

But as far as he was concerned, attending an event to

celebrate the arrival of his friend's baby went above and beyond. Since when did guys attend baby showers?

"Are you absolutely certain I need to be here?" he asked as he pulled the Mercedes next to Travis's minivan.

"It's a barbecue."

"It's a baby shower."

"It's a baby celebration," she clarified. "Granted, Cole and Meg's baby is already here. But she arrived before Meg's friends had a chance to throw her a shower."

"Tell me there won't be games."

"No games."

His expression was clearly skeptical.

Poppy laughed. "I honestly don't know if there will be games. But if there are, you won't be alone in your misery."

If anyone had told Dr. Ben Campbell that on a late July day he'd be attending a baby shower, he'd have told them they were crazy. But he liked Cole Lassiter, liked the way he and Meg had dropped everything that was going on in their lives several years earlier to return to Jackson Hole and raise the son of mutual friends who'd died in a car accident.

Charlie had to be eight or nine now. And he vaguely remembered hearing something about the boy being Cole's biological son, but that could have simply been a rumor. Now, there was a little girl in their lives, born six weeks ago.

Ben lifted the trunk and pulled out the gift Poppy had purchased for the baby. The pink frilly bag was bad enough, but there was also an oversize ribbon tied to the handle, in pink naturally. Inside was an assortment of baby items.

Soon he'd have to know how to use such baby items, he reminded himself. The rest of Poppy's pregnancy would go quickly and he needed to be prepared. *They* needed to be prepared.

She slipped her arm through his. "Why so solemn?"

"I don't even know what most of the stuff in this bag is for…and yet this fall, you and I, we're going to have to know."

"It scares me sometimes, too. But we'll be okay. I mean, we're smart people. We're responsible adults. We'll be good parents."

"We will," he reassured her. "And if we have questions—"

"We'll ask your parents. Or mine. Or our friends." Poppy paused as if she liked the sound of the words. "You know it's weird, you and I having a group of friends we both enjoy."

He lifted a brow as they sauntered up the sidewalk toward the large two-story stone home. "What's odd about that?"

Poppy's eyes grew thoughtful. "I tried to like Bill's friends but I couldn't."

"Why not?" While Ben enjoyed it when Poppy shared information about her past, he didn't like it so much when she brought up Bill.

"Most of them didn't respect their marriage vows any more than he did." She shook her head, as if she still found it difficult to believe. "Several propositioned me in my own home."

Ben was still trying to decide how to respond to that when the front door swung open and Cole called out a greeting. They'd barely stepped into the foyer when Meg joined them.

"Here she is." Cole smiled when Meg handed him the baby wrapped in a hot pink blanket. "This is Evie."

Poppy stepped forward and with one finger, pushed back the blanket to get a better view of the baby. Creamy white skin and a tuft of hair with a reddish tinge. Her eyes were closed and her little rosebud of a mouth sucked contentedly on nothing.

"She's gorgeous." Poppy breathed the words. "May I hold her?"

"Of course." With great gentleness Cole settled the baby in Poppy's arms.

Her face lit up with pleasure. For an instant the baby

fussed but when Poppy made little cooing noises, Evie relaxed.

"What does big brother think of her?" Poppy asked.

"Adores her." Meg smiled. "And he's such a good helper."

With the baby still cradled in her arms, Poppy followed Cole and Meg onto the back terrace. Though the event had been billed as a baby celebration and barbecue, the feel of an old-fashioned baby shower was very much in evidence.

The trees surrounding the patio were decorated with oversize shiny pink ornaments as well as lights in the softest shade of pink. Someone had draped a banner between several trees which proclaimed Welcome, Evie.

A table off to the right held a mountain of gifts, most wrapped in various shades of pink.

"I'm going to drop off our present." Ben gave her arm a squeeze. "Be right back."

But ten minutes later, when the baby had long been transferred to another woman's arms and everyone was grabbing the burgers and bratwursts from Ryan and Nick at the monster grill, Poppy found herself alone.

"When I saw all the pink, I seriously considered turning around."

Poppy turned toward the familiar voice. Handsome, as always, in jeans and a white shirt open at the neck, Winn Ferris stood surveying the crowd before him like a king overlooking his kingdom.

"Mitzi dragged me here," he said, in answer to her unspoken question, handing her an iced tea.

She closed her fingers around the glass. "I thought she was dating Kelvin Reed."

"Still is." Winn took a pull from the bottle of beer. "Apparently he had to fly back to Denver."

Poppy turned in the direction of his gaze and saw Ben standing by his pretty colleague next to the tower of presents. Always the fashionista, Mitzi wore skinny jeans tucked into cowboy boots with blocks of turquoise and a white cowboy shirt with thin lines of turquoise and pearl buttons.

Today her hair had a decidedly reddish cast. Part of it was pulled up while the rest hung to her shoulders. She looked simply adorable, Poppy thought with a sigh.

Based on the single-mindedness of his attention, Ben had also noticed.

"I always wondered why they broke up," Winn said in a low tone.

Poppy was tempted to ignore the comment. But this was the father of her baby they were discussing, a fact Winn undoubtedly knew quite well.

"It's not easy to know what goes on in any relationship." Her voice turned cool. "Why some stay together while others break up."

"You're in love with him."

"Ben and I are living together," she said, neither confirming nor denying his words. "This fall we'll have a baby together."

"You're no pushover."

"What's that supposed to mean?"

"I think you've got what it takes to make a relationship work." Winn glanced back at Mitzi and Ben. "As long as the other partner is equally committed."

"I don't know the first thing about throwing a baby shower, Ben," Mitzi protested, appearing stunned by his suggestion. "I'm fairly certain one of Poppy's friends will end up throwing her one, anyway."

"I want to make sure she has one," Ben said stubbornly. "It'll be a nice surprise."

"Does she like surprises?"

"Don't most women? I know she likes this kind of stuff."

While Ben liked a party as much as the next guy, he'd never understand the appeal of baby showers. Yet, he'd heard the excitement in Poppy's voice when she'd spoken of this barbecue. *Barbecue.* He snorted. Putting that name on it was merely a way to entice men to an event they'd never otherwise attend.

When he'd asked if she was going to have a barbecue, er, shower, the light in her eyes had dimmed. She'd told him no, that she really hadn't been back all that long and that throwing a shower was something usually done by old friends.

He'd told her they could throw one at his house. There was plenty of room. And household staff could see to the details.

Appearing quite horrified, she'd told him that simply wasn't done. Though he hadn't fully grasped the logic, he'd backed off. Until he'd seen Mitzi.

"Well…" Mitzi twirled a piece of her hair around her fingers, a thoughtful look on her face. "I suppose I could throw one for her. Kate would help me."

"Good."

"Kate likes Poppy," Mitzi added. "For that matter, I do, too. You know she's a much better match for you than I ever was."

"I agree."

"Just like that?" she teased. "No denials?"

He laughed. "No reason to deny. Poppy and I are good together."

"You're in love with her."

He froze.

Mitzi's vivid blue eyes turned sharp and assessing. Her lips lifted in a catlike smile.

"I see it in your stunned expression," she pressed, as if delighted to catch him off balance. "You're crazy, stupid in love with her."

Crazy, stupid.

Ben straightened, his shoulders suddenly stiff. "I'll never be crazy, stupid in love with anyone."

Not again, he thought. Never again.

"Yeah, right." Mitzi's eyes danced. "Tell that to some-one who'll believe it."

"Thanks, Winn." Poppy took a sip of the iced tea he'd brought her.

If she were on her own, she'd be mingling, talking with fellow book club members. She'd be doing something be-sides waiting for Ben to quit laughing and talking with Mitzi. But Winn showed no inclination to move on and she couldn't really walk away. Not with his "date" currently preoccupied with her "date."

Just when Poppy decided she and Winn had exhausted the small talk, Ben and Mitzi sauntered over. Mitzi seemed in high spirits and her blue eyes gleamed. After greeting Poppy, she tucked her arm through Winn's and they headed for the bar.

Ben's eyes now held shadows. Poppy was curious what he and Mitzi had discussed. She wondered if he'd tell her.

"I was surprised to see Mitzi here with Winn," she said, offering him an opening. "He told me Kelvin was out of town."

"Kelvin is just another momentary distraction for her." Ben smiled, suddenly all solicitous. "Are you hungry? Would you like a burger?"

Quit worrying, Poppy told herself. Be fearless. Be spon-taneous. "I'd like a bratwurst."

The look in his eyes turned teasing. "The lady has de-cided to live dangerously."

Poppy started to smile, and abruptly straightened. Her hand moved to her belly. "Oh."

Concern blanketed Ben's face. "What is it?"

"The baby moved." She gazed at him, her eyes filled with awe. "It *does* feel like butterfly wings."

Seeing the look of wonder on her face, unable to stop the

warm tide of emotion welling up inside him, Ben admitted Mitzi had been right. He was in love with Poppy.

He wasn't crazy, stupid in love, he told himself quite firmly. But definitely in love.

With a feeling of rightness, he placed his palm protectively on her belly…and felt a kick.

Chapter Nineteen

By the time they returned to Ben's home that evening, Poppy was ready to relax. Groucho greeted them at the door with short staccato barks.

"Hey, boy." Poppy scrubbed the top of his soft furry head. "Miss us?"

Ben liked the sound of the "us" even though Mitzi's words kept echoing in his head. He wasn't crazy, stupid in love with Poppy, he told himself again. He loved her. But he wasn't stupid about it.

He pointed in the direction of the sofa. "Take a seat in the living room."

"Ooh, so masterful." A tiny smile hovered on the corners of her lips. "What do you have planned?"

"Trust me."

Poppy did as he asked, glancing over her shoulder as she strolled down the hall.

Once in the kitchen Ben pulled out two wineglasses and filled them with sparkling grape juice. He told himself to not make such a big deal out of something that happened to millions of women every day.

But not to his woman.

And that was the crux of the matter. Poppy was his woman. This was his baby.

He carried the glasses into the living room where she sat on the sofa, petting Groucho. The dog leaped to the floor as if shot from a cannon.

"I'm sorry," Poppy began. "I keep forgetting you don't like him on the—"

She stopped speaking and her mouth formed a perfect O.

He handed her a glass, then took a seat beside her. "Feeling our baby move for the first time is a momentous occasion. It deserves a toast."

Pleasure filled Poppy's eyes and he knew he'd made the right decision in bringing out the sparkling juice. She glanced down at the glass.

"Sparkling grape juice, now." He clinked his glass against hers. "Champagne, after the baby is born."

She took a sip then placed her glass on the coffee table. With one fluid movement, she wrapped her arms around his neck. "Thank you so much for this. It's so sweet."

She buried her face against his neck and he inhaled the clean fresh scent of her.

He wrapped his arms around her. "I'm glad you're here with me."

She lifted her gaze. "Me, too."

"I love you, Poppy," he said, the words coming more easily than he'd imagined.

She slid her fingers into his hair. "I love you, too."

Once again his lips found hers and she forgot how to think, how to breathe. Her shirt had already found its way to the floor and his fingers were on her bra clasp when her phone began a tinny rendition of "New York, New York."

"Ignore it."

"That song plays for any 212 area code." She leaned over

and picked up the phone. "My great-aunt Katherine lives in the city. She hasn't been well."

He dropped his hands while Poppy pressed the phone against her ear. "Hello."

Ben sat back and sipped the grape juice. His eyes narrowed as her expression changed. At first he'd thought something bad had indeed happened to her aunt. Then he heard her say a name. *Bill.*

"I can't believe you lied to me about that." Poppy paused, took a breath. "Scratch that. I can believe it. But I never thought you'd have stooped that low."

Her face was now set in hard planes, her wide and generous mouth, a thin line. Her ex must have had a lot to say because for a long while it seemed all she did was listen.

"Well, I'm happy for you. Who knew telling me all this would make you feel better." The sarcasm in Poppy's voice came through loud and clear. She listened for a few more minutes, made a few noises of acknowledgment then hung up.

"Dirty rotten liar." She rose to her feet and began to pace. "I can't believe he expected me to just forgive him. Yeah, right. It'll be a cold day in hell before that happens."

Groucho sat on the floor, his head turning from side to side as she continued to pace.

"Come and sit with me," Ben said in a soothing tone. "Tell me what he said. Then I'll go to Manhattan and beat him up."

As he hoped, that brought a smile to her lips. "Would you really do that?"

"Sweetheart, I'd do just about anything for you."

Poppy returned to the sofa. "I suppose I should be grateful to him for solving yet another mystery."

Though Ben wasn't thirsty, he downed the rest of the grape juice and waited. She'd tell him what had gotten her so riled up when she was ready.

"Bill is doing a twelve-step program for sex addiction."

He lifted a brow.

"Apparently he's at the stage where you're supposed to contact all the people you've wronged and ask for forgiveness."

When she didn't continue, Ben took her hand, found it ice cold. "Did he ask you to forgive him for cheating on you?"

"Ohmigod, he never mentioned the cheating." She gave a helpless sounding laugh, and pulled her hand from his. "Why doesn't that surprise me? His list of transgressions probably runs into the thousands. It's probably hard for him to keep them all straight."

"Why did he call?" Ben asked, now perplexed.

"To tell me he was sorry for not letting me know that he was sterile and that's why I couldn't get pregnant."

"I thought he'd fathered a couple of kids," Ben said, trying to remember exactly what Poppy had told him.

"He did. Shortly after the second was born, he apparently had a vasectomy. A fact he failed to mention before we married or when I was undergoing all those procedures to find out what was wrong with me." Poppy's hands clenched and unclenched in her lap. "I should have been suspicious when the urologist dictated a letter instead of sending the semen analysis. But the doctor was a friend of his and I thought it was nice he went to the extra effort."

She took a deep breath, then let it out slowly. "I was so gullible, so foolish."

"I don't like it that he hurt you."

She searched his gaze and what she found there must have reassured her of his sincerity, because she rested her head on his shoulder. "Thanks for that."

After a moment, he brushed a kiss across her lips and stood, holding out a hand to her. "Come with me. I know something that will make you feel better."

She let him pull her to standing and cocked her head.

"A massage. Guaranteed to obliterate any tension or your money back."

Her eyes gleamed with suspicion. "I read somewhere that ninety-six percent of back rubs not done in hospitals or medical clinics lead to sex."

"Really?" Ben wiggled his eyebrows. "Now those are the kind of odds I like."

Sunday dinner at the Campbell ranch was always a relaxing affair. The more Poppy got to know Ben's mother and dad, the more she liked them. They could laugh and talk about practically any topic.

But when Ben's mother asked her what they'd done the previous evening, Poppy found herself blushing. Thankfully, Ben saved her when he mentioned the movie they'd watched.

Of course he didn't mention that had been after the back rub, after they'd made love for hours. By the time she was back on the sofa with a bowl of popcorn in her lap, another glass of sparkling grape juice in her hand and Ben on one side of her and Groucho on the other, she'd been totally relaxed and her conversation with Bill had seemed like a bad dream.

"Why don't we retire to the living room for coffee and dessert?" Dori said.

Poppy pushed back from her chair. "I'll help clear the table."

"No, dear." Taking her arm, Dori propelled her into the living room. "I have a surprise for you."

Ben cast a suspicious glance at the stacks of albums positioned on a low table. "What are those?"

His father lifted his hands in a gesture of surrender. "I had nothing to do with any of this."

Ben shot his mother a questioning glance.

"Pictures. I thought Poppy might enjoy looking at ones of you growing up." Dori took a seat on the sofa and patted a spot next to her. "Poppy, you sit here."

"I'm surprised you didn't bring out the videos," Ben muttered.

"Don't tempt her," John warned.

"I'm saving those for another visit," Dori said cheerily, pulling a giant album onto her lap and flipping it open.

The key-lime cheesecake had been polished off by the time they reached Ben's college years. He'd tried to put a stop to the viewing several times, insisting it was getting late. But Poppy demurred. Apparently she enjoyed seeing him with missing teeth and haircuts that had once been stylish but now looked ridiculous.

"This is Ben and Kristin." Dori pointed to a picture of her son with one arm looped over the shoulders of a tall blonde with a friendly smile. What looked to be a university building loomed large behind them. "They were together during his medical school years but went their separate ways shortly before graduation. I never did understand what happened there."

Dori turned to her son.

Poppy expected him to make some lighthearted joke like he'd done about the other girls in previous pictures, but when he hesitated, she realized this one had been different. She'd mattered.

"Kris found someone else," Ben said in a matter-of-fact tone. "I believe she's practicing in San Antonio. Or maybe it's Austin."

They continued through the rest the album then called it a night. Poppy waited until they were home before she brought up Kris. "You were in love with her. The girl in the picture."

He gave a casual shrug. "That was a long time ago."

"You were in love with her," Poppy repeated.

He took her jacket and hung it up. Then he paused, as if he had to think about the answer. "Yes."

Poppy forced a casual tone. "What happened?"

"After medical school, we went our separate ways."

And that, Poppy thought, told her absolutely nothing.

"But if you loved her and she loved you—" Poppy paused, then recognized the look in his eyes. "She didn't love you."

"I thought she did, but she didn't." He wandered into the kitchen, added water to Groucho's bowl.

She stood in the doorway, an uneasy feeling in the pit of her stomach. "What happened?"

For a moment, she wasn't sure he would tell her. But after giving Groucho a doggie treat, he rested his back against the counter and met her gaze. "During our last year in med school, she dumped me for someone else. I found out later she'd been seeing him behind my back."

His lips lifted in a humorless smile.

Poppy thought of Bill. She remembered how she'd felt when a "friend" had finally told her the truth. "That had to have been devastating."

"We weren't married, Poppy," he said as if that made a difference.

"What does that matter? You loved her. Trusted her. And she betrayed you."

"Yes, she did." His jaw set in a hard angle. "But I was foolish. I gave her my heart, my whole heart."

For someone who had been doing a good job tracking the conversation, Poppy felt as if she'd suddenly taken a wrong turn. "Why was that foolish?"

"Because when you love someone that deeply, it gives them power over you," he said. "I should have kept a part of myself back. I won't make that mistake again."

The next day, instead of concentrating on her work, Poppy found herself pondering Ben's words. When she'd married Bill, she'd given him her whole heart. He'd deliberately held part of himself back from her.

Though she knew Ben hadn't done that with her, his attitude troubled her. Because she loved him.

He said he loved her.

But how much?

She shoved the thought aside. Grabbing another cup of coffee, she returned to her desk and refocused on the computer screen.

It was another paperwork day and she was determined to get caught up. She'd always prided herself on staying on top of the reports that the courts demanded, but lately an overabundance of fieldwork had left little time for documentation.

Her stomach had just begun to growl when there was a rap at the office door. "Come in."

She looked up. Her heart gave a little leap when she saw Ben.

"What are you doing here?" she asked.

"Not quite the greeting I expected," he said with an easy smile. "Perhaps this will change it."

She surveyed the brown paper bag dangling from his fingers. "What's in it?"

"Only a chicken salad sandwich with cranberries and walnuts on wheatberry bread. With an apple. And a fruitbar." He smiled. "From the Green Gateau."

Her favorite sandwich from her favorite restaurant.

She reached for the sack but he moved it back at the last second.

He moved to sit casually on the corner of her desk, the bag swinging from his fingers. "There's a catch."

Poppy heaved an exaggerated sigh, but couldn't keep the smile from her lips. "Of course, there is."

"The park. Lunch. With me."

Poppy glanced at the clock. "I can take my lunch now. But do you have time?"

He waved a dismissive hand. "My first surgery got cancelled. Patient came down with a gastrointestinal bug during the night."

Poppy pushed back her chair, rose to her feet and, quick as a cobra, snatched the sack from his hands. "You've got a deal."

With one hand she kept the sack close, with the other, she smoothed down the bright blue top she wore over her growing baby bump.

Ben was seized suddenly with the urge to pull her close, to wrap his arms around her and never let her go. His surprise at the sheer force of such an emotion, made his tone a bit brusque. "We'd best get going."

"There's one thing I need to do first." Poppy set the sack aside, wrapped her arms around his neck and pulled him close for a deep lingering kiss.

"Wow," he said as she stepped back, picked up the sack and shot him a saucy smile. "That was quite an appetizer."

"Unfortunately this—" Poppy tapped a finger against the sack "—will have to be the main course. Now this evening—"

Ben thought about the meeting he'd set with Mitzi. "I'm going to be a little late getting home tonight."

She lifted a shoulder in a slight shrug. "Your loss."

"Not that late." He took her arm as they strolled out into the bright sunshine. "Just don't wait on me for dinner."

"What's going on?"

"Meeting," he said and changed the subject.

"You know," he said later as they sat on the park bench and watched several preschool-age children play on the equipment, "in several years it'll be our kid standing on the top of the slide about to fall."

As they watched, a frantic mother hurried over and made the little girl sit on her bottom.

Poppy's eyes took on a faraway look. "I wanted a child for so long. Now it's actually going to happen."

He took a gulp of soda. It was hard to believe that in a few short months, he was going to be someone's dad.

Ben pulled his attention back to Poppy when she placed a hand on his arm.

"I know when you asked me out on Valentine's Day,

you weren't planning on becoming a father by the end of the year."

"Life often takes unexpected turns." Ben's gaze shifted back to the children. "But I like the idea of having a child. And, you certainly deserve to be a mother. You'll be a good one."

She swallowed the last bite of her sandwich. "I believe that's one of the nicest things anyone has ever said to me."

"It's the truth," Ben said matter-of-factly. "If I would have set out to choose a mother for my child, I couldn't have found anyone better than you."

Her eyes swam with sudden tears. "I couldn't have picked a better father for my child than you."

"Our child," he said pointedly, covering her hand with his.

And then he kissed her.

She wrapped her arms around his neck, reveling in the closeness until his pager went off. Minutes later, he was headed to the hospital.

Because she still had time on her break, Poppy stayed on the park bench, feeling the warmth of the wooden slats through the thin cotton of her shirt. She popped the last bite of the apricot and date fruit bar into her mouth then washed it down with iced tea.

Laughter rang out as children played, free from the cares of the world.

Freedom was the word she'd chosen at the book club.

What did it mean to her?

The freedom to let go of the past and embrace the future?

The freedom to love Ben Campbell fully and build a family with him?

Though Ben hadn't asked her to marry him, she'd sensed the words poised on his lips several times lately.

Perhaps when he did ask, she'd say yes.

With a suddenly light heart, Poppy strolled back to the office.

Chapter Twenty

Since Ben had a meeting, Poppy stayed at the office to finish up some paperwork. With music blasting in the background, she munched on apple wedges and stayed focused. When she finally glanced at the clock, she was stunned. It was nearly eight o'clock.

While her computer powered down, Poppy pulled on her jacket and called Ben. He answered on the third ring. "I'm sorry I forgot to call," she said quickly. "I lost track of the time. I'm on my way now."

"Actually, I'm not home, either." He sounded distracted. "I should be there shortly."

Was that music she heard in the background? "Where are you?"

"Just finishing up some business," he said smoothly. "I won't be long. Drive carefully."

"Yeah," she said, "You, too."

Frowning, she clicked off, her trouble antennae quivering. Even as anxiety gripped her chest, she reminded herself that Ben wasn't Bill. Tonight, while they relaxed in the living room with a cup of cocoa, she'd ask about his evening.

Ben would explain where he'd been and what he'd been doing. She'd do the same. He'd laugh when he heard how she'd gotten caught up in boring paperwork. She'd laugh when she realized she'd worried over nothing.

Since there was no need to hurry home, Poppy took a detour to Hill of Beans, intending to grab a decaf cappuccino. She was sitting at a stoplight when she saw Ben.

Poppy gripped the steering wheel so tightly her knuckles turned white. The man she loved was with his former lover...and they'd just left the Red Sands Hotel.

Her blood froze as Ben gave the stylish doctor a quick hug and whispered something in her ear. As she watched, Mitzi laughed and tossed her tousled mane of hair provocatively before sashaying down the street.

For a second Poppy feared Ben would turn and see her. Then she wished he would. But he was too focused on his pretty colleague.

The car behind Poppy honked and she realized the light had changed. She hit the accelerator, but had to pull over several blocks later because she had difficulty seeing the road. It was hard to see anything through the curtain of tears blurring her vision.

Poppy pounded her fist against the steering wheel and swallowed a scream. Ben had assured her it was over between him and Mitzi. He'd insisted there was nothing but work between them. Yet, he was still seeing her. Still having sex with her. What else explained the two of them together at a hotel?

As sobs rose in her throat, she pushed them down.

Poppy had listened to Bill's lies, believed his excuses. She'd trusted him because that's what you were supposed to do in a committed relationship.

She'd done the same with Ben. She'd given him her trust. She'd overlooked him having lunch with Mitzi at Hill of

Beans. Even explained away the attention he'd paid to Mitzi at the baby celebration and now...

Now it ended.

Wiping away the tears, Poppy squared her shoulders. Her penchant for being a trusting fool stopped today.

Ben found himself smiling as he pulled the Mercedes into the garage. It had been an extremely productive evening. Since he couldn't hold a surprise baby shower for Poppy at his place and Mitzi insisted her condo wasn't large enough, she'd suggested the Red Sands Hotel. Apparently she'd attended a bridal shower there and found the food and atmosphere top-notch.

After seeing the place, Ben concurred. Tonight they'd gotten the ball rolling thanks to Andrea, the hotel's event planner. Ben hadn't considered Poppy might like her mother and sister to attend until Mitzi suggested it. He had both of their phone numbers so Mitzi offered to contact them to see what weekend would work best.

All Ben had to do was keep his mouth shut about the arrangements. He grinned, already envisioning Poppy's reaction the day she walked into the hotel and found friends and family gathered there.

With the bouquet of wildflowers he'd picked up at the florist's in hand, Ben opened the door. His smile disappeared at the sight of Poppy standing in the foyer, her eyes red-rimmed and puffy.

He saw the luggage at her feet and immediately thought of her parents. "Your mom and dad. Has something happened?"

"They're fine." Poppy closed her eyes, breathed deep. "They're all fine."

Relief flooded him, followed quickly by confusion. Clearly something had upset her. If not her family...

He was almost at her side when her eyes flashed open.

Only then did he see it wasn't sadness in her gaze, but anger. Not grief on her face, but restrained fury.

"Sweetheart." Ben inched closer, tentative and cautious, as if crossing a lake of ice that had begun to crack. When he reached out to her, he realized he still held the bouquet. "I brought you flowers."

"Bill used to bring me flowers." Her voice was bleak, as empty and flat as her expression. "I didn't figure it out until after we split."

"Do we really need to discuss your ex—"

"He'd bring them to me after he'd been with another woman." Poppy gave a humorless laugh. "I received lots of flowers from him. Now, I'm getting them from you. Ironic, huh?"

"Poppy—" He gentled his tone. "What's going on here?"

"I'm moving out. Moving back to my apartment." She trailed off and he watched her struggle for composure as her eyes went shiny with tears.

"Why would you do that?" Ben kept his voice calm, his tone conversational, even though his palms had begun to sweat. "Talk to me."

"Where were you tonight?"

The question came out of left field, taking Ben by surprise. He hesitated only a second, but it was long enough to unleash her fury.

"Let me answer." Her voice now held a steely edge. "You spent the evening with your former lover."

Ben stilled. She'd seen him and Mitzi together? At the hotel?

Dammit. Dammit. Dammit.

Should he tell her about the shower? Blow the surprise? He saw no other option.

"I can explain everything." Keeping his gaze firmly locked on hers, Ben spread out his hands. "Just listen—"

"Listen to you lie?" Poppy's lips lifted in what could

only be called a sneer and her tone turned flippant. "Sorry. Not in the mood."

"Why would you think I'd lie?" Ben asked, his own anger bubbling just below the surface. Then it hit him. She thought he'd cheated on her. With Mitzi. "I'm not your ex-husband, Poppy. And frankly, I resent the comparison."

"He never loved me completely," she murmured almost to herself. "If at all. Just like you."

The pain in her voice softened some of his anger.

Still, none of this made any sense. What was she talking about? Hadn't he told her, shown her that she meant everything to him? He opened his mouth to speak, then remembered the comment he'd made weeks ago about not loving any woman too much. A comment she seemed determined to shove in his face to hide her own lack of commitment.

Ben gestured toward the luggage. "You've been itching for a reason to walk out on me."

Her face paled. "That's not true."

"Then let me explain why I was with Mitzi tonight."

"It doesn't take a rocket scientist to figure that one out," she muttered.

"You think you know so much." He stunned them both by flinging the bouquet across the coffee table, scattering the pretty flowers.

He watched Poppy's color drain, saw her take a step back. *Get it under control,* he told himself.

"You've had your say." Ben took a steadying breath. "Now grant me the same courtesy. If you're determined to leave after I finish, I'll load your suitcases in the car myself."

Poppy rubbed the back of her neck and nodded, looking incredibly weary. "Okay."

"We can go into the living room," he began. "You can sit—"

"No." She brushed the suggestion aside with a flick of her hand. "I'm fine here."

Ben shifted from one foot to the other. How had things gotten so screwed up? He didn't even like baby showers.

"I now realize withholding information from you was a mistake. I should have been up-front about what I was doing and where I was tonight." Ben kept his gaze on her face. "I just wanted the baby shower to be a surprise."

"Baby shower?" Her voice broke on the words.

His lips curved a little. "I approached Mitzi about hosting one for you when we were at Cole's house."

She drew in a shuddering breath. "Why her?"

"I wasn't sure which of your friends to ask. Planning a shower seemed a big responsibility. So I decided to ask the one person I knew wouldn't feel obligated to do it simply because I asked. Mitzi would only agree if it was something she wanted to do."

"She's doing it for you."

Ben's gray eyes softened. "She didn't agree for my sake, but for yours. Mitzi genuinely likes you."

Poppy felt the first tingle of relief loosen the fist around her heart. Surely his current lover wouldn't want to throw his baby mama a party?

She wanted to believe Ben. Dear God, how she wanted to believe him. But she remembered her ex and his very plausible explanations. "I saw you and Mitzi coming out of a *hotel*."

"I told her we could have the party here, but she insisted that wouldn't be appropriate. And she thought her condo was too small." His voice took on a clip of annoyance. "She'd attended a wedding shower at the hotel and was impressed. This evening we met with the hotel's event manager. The woman gave me her card. You can call her if you feel the need to verify what I've told you is accurate."

Poppy wished she could simply take what he said on faith, but she knew if she didn't verify his story the doubts would fester. She held out a hand. "Thank you."

With business card in hand, she dialed the cell number. By the time Poppy ended the call, her doubts had been erased, replaced by regret that she'd hurt him.

"I don't know what to say, other than when you've been lied to so often, it's difficult to trust. Even when you desperately want to trust." She felt her cheeks warm. "I falsely accused you. I'm truly sorry."

"I know you've been hurt, but I'm not Bill. And like I said before, I resent the comparisons." She could see his jaw tighten and noticed the control it took for him to relax it again. "I would never cheat on you or hurt you like he did. In the future, if something comes up that worries you, I ask that you give me a chance to explain before jumping to conclusions and thinking the worst of me."

The way he said the words, the look in his eyes, shredded her control. As tears slipped down her cheeks, all she could manage in response was a jerky nod.

Blowing out a harsh breath, he drew her to him and simply held her.

Poppy leaned into the embrace, let herself be absorbed and comforted by his warmth, his touch. She always felt safe and loved in his arms. "I love you," she murmured.

"I love you," he replied, now gently stroking her back.

It's enough, Poppy told herself.

But even when his lips lowered to hers in an achingly tender kiss, Poppy found herself wondering just how much he loved her. With his whole heart? With every fiber of his being? She thought about asking him, but knew these kinds of questions couldn't be answered with words.

And if she eventually concluded he didn't love her totally, it would be for her to decide if only owning part of his heart would be enough.

As Ben held Poppy tight against him that night, he realized how close he'd come to losing it all. He'd been a fool to think he could put strict parameters on his feelings. The fear in his gut had made him realize that nothing was more important to him than her and their unborn baby.

He'd fallen in love. Totally. Completely.

There wasn't anything he wouldn't do for her, for their child. If she left him...

His heart stopped beating for several seconds before he was able to reassure himself that wouldn't happen. He wouldn't let it happen. For the rest of her life he'd make Poppy so happy she couldn't imagine being anywhere but with him.

Several months later, with Jackson Hole firmly in the throes of an Indian summer, Ben arrived home on a Saturday afternoon to a strange car in the driveway and the sound of feminine laughter coming from the deck around back.

After stowing his workout gear, he grabbed a beer from the refrigerator then decided to see who Poppy was entertaining today. Through the kitchen window he saw Cassidy and Hailey sitting around the patio table with a very pregnant Poppy. Groucho slept at her feet. Large glasses of iced tea and a tray of assorted fresh fruits, artfully arranged by Angela, were on the table.

He paused, trying to remember if Poppy had mentioned the two would be visiting today. Not that it mattered. After all, this was her home, too. Or, he hoped she thought of it that way. The fact that she continued to pay rent on her apartment was troubling.

What bothered him even more was the couple of times she'd casually alluded to the possibility of moving back there after the baby was born. He'd made it clear that he wanted her to stay. That he wanted them to be a family.

He'd brought up marriage. Though she hadn't said no, she hadn't said yes. Actually, she'd acted like it was some sort of joke and quickly changed the subject.

Because Ben knew she'd been burned by marriage, he

hadn't pressed. But it chapped his thighs. He wasn't Bill and she should darn well know that by now. Should know *him*.

After many sleepless nights, he concluded that she still believed he didn't love her enough. That was the only possible explanation and it gibed with what she'd said to him the night she'd accused him of sleeping with Mitzi.

Ben tried telling her that she was his whole world, but words were, well, simply words. He wished he could figure out a way to convince her he was sincere.

"Did you hear the Jaycees are trying to recruit men for the Torch Singing competition next Valentine's Day?" Cassidy spoke loudly, her words clearly audible through the partially opened window.

Ben took a long pull of beer and thanked God he wouldn't be one of those men. He meant it when he'd told Poppy after her stellar Valentine's Day performance that she'd never see him on a stage.

Hailey said something in a low tone that made the other women laugh.

The fact she and Hailey were now friends had made Poppy happy. She'd been determined to make things right with the perky blonde and Hailey had finally responded to her overtures. She'd even apologized to Poppy for being such a "brat."

Smiling, Ben pulled a bag of chips from the cupboard. Jalapeño ranch, his favorite treat after a strenuous workout.

"Are you kidding?" Poppy laughed. "Ben would never get up on stage."

Ben's ears perked up at the sound of his name.

"You know me so well." He grinned and dumped a mound of chips on a plate.

"I bet he would if you asked him."

Cassidy again, Ben thought with a scowl. The woman should learn to keep her mouth shut.

"Don't you think it'd be romantic?" Cassidy continued. "Having Ben on a stage, singing a love song to you?"

Hailey said something again, and through the window Ben saw Poppy nod.

"It would be very romantic," Poppy agreed. "But I can't think of anything that would cause him to put himself out there like that."

"Remember when Tripp proposed to Anna at the fashion show last year?" Cassidy exhaled a heartfelt sigh. "I almost started crying when he got down on one knee. It was so doggone sweet."

"Yes, but Tripp is…" Poppy began then paused. "Totally in love with Anna."

Hailey spoke again, but even when he took a step closer to the window, Ben couldn't hear what she said. But when Poppy spoke, he heard all too clearly.

"No." Poppy shook her head. "Not Ben. Never. Not in a million years."

Chapter Twenty-One

"Seriously? You're wearing *that* tonight?" Hailey wrinkled her nose.

"Way too boring," Cassidy agreed.

Poppy felt her cheeks warm as she glanced down at what she'd chosen for their "girls' night out." Granted, the outfit wasn't cutting edge but the pants were this season's style and the bulky cable-knit sweater had been a recent gift from Ben's mother.

"What do you expect me to wear?" She gave a little laugh. "A party dress?"

Hailey and Cassidy exchanged glances.

"How about that pretty red one you wore to church last Sunday?" Hailey suggested.

"Didn't you tell me Ben loves it when you wear red?" Cassidy twisted a strand of hair that could only be described as the color of a blood orange around one finger.

"Ben won't be with us tonight," Poppy reminded her friends. "He and Tripp have plans."

"Oh, he'll see it." Hailey's eyes sparkled.

Poppy raised a brow.

"When you get home," Hailey said quickly, pink staining her cheeks. "You know, when he takes it off."

Poppy chuckled, realizing it was probably how the evening would play out. Despite her growing belly, Ben's desire for her hadn't showed signs of waning.

"Besides, we got dressed up." Cassidy gave Poppy a little push in the direction of the bedroom. "You don't want to be the only slacker."

Poppy started to say something about neither of them being all that fancy, then realized both women were wearing dresses. Hailey had on a lilac-colored sweater dress with heeled boots. Cassidy had chosen an eye-popping gold wrap dress that—depending on perspective—either clashed or complimented the new color of her hair.

They *had* dressed up. And she, who'd spent most of her life noticing fashion, had been more focused on the evening ahead and the fun awaiting her, than on clothing.

Progress, she thought.

"We want this to be a special night," Hailey ventured when Poppy made no move toward the bedroom she shared with Ben. At Poppy's questioning glance, she smiled. "Your little man is due in less than four weeks. This might be the last time the three of us will be able to go out like this for quite a while."

"You're right." An upsurge of emotion made Poppy's voice thick. "I'll change."

Poppy stripped off her pants and sweater then carefully removed the red maternity dress from the hanger. Her lips lifted. Ben had insisted she buy something new for a party they'd attended last month. How her life had changed. She'd been to more social events—and enjoyed them all—in the past six months than she had in the prior two years.

Last year, she'd been alone on Thanksgiving and Christmas. This year, because the baby would be too small to travel, her family and Ben's family would be celebrating the holidays at their, er, Ben's house.

She'd decided to wait until after the first of the year to decide about moving back to her apartment with the baby. Even if they didn't live together, she and Ben and their son would always be a family.

Not in the traditional sense, of course. There would be no wedding rings on their fingers but it wasn't because Ben hadn't asked.

It was her hang-up. She knew it. Accepted it. But couldn't get past it.

Ben told her daily he cared. She believed he loved her. It was the *how much* she couldn't keep from questioning. Perhaps she should settle for what he had to give. She'd been tempted to do just that many times.

But while she hadn't been able to make herself walk away, neither would she allow herself to settle. Or to allow him to settle. Didn't everyone deserve to be with someone who loved them—and who they loved—totally and completely?

"What the heck are you doing up there? Sewing the dress yourself?" Cassidy's loud voice carried easily from the bottom of the stairs. "Get a move on. We're going to miss the first set."

Poppy quickly slipped on the dress and shoes then, on impulse, spritzed on perfume. And, feeling spontaneous, grabbed the sparkly headband she hadn't worn since last spring. A touch of cherry red lipstick and she was ready to party.

"I didn't even know The Flying Crane was open on Monday night," Poppy said to Cassidy as they walked through the door of the club.

"I told you, this is the place to be tonight." Cassidy tossed the words over her shoulder as Hailey and Poppy followed her through the maze of tables to a small round one next to the stage.

"I can't believe we found an empty table." Poppy took a seat and Hailey pulled out the chair next to her while Cassidy hurried off to get the drinks.

"Some things are meant to be." Hailey lifted a hand in a wave.

Poppy followed the direction of her friend's gaze and saw Winn Ferris seated at the bar. She didn't know why it surprised her to see him. The place was filled with people she knew. "Tell me about the guy who'll be performing. He must be popular to have drawn in so many people on a Monday night."

"He's a new artist. I've never heard him sing, but I'm jazzed about the performance." Hailey laid her hand over Poppy's. "I know I've said this before, but I'm really happy about you and Ben being together."

"Thank you." Poppy cleared her throat, touched by the young woman's obvious sincerity.

"When he looks at you—" Hailey shivered "—I get goose bumps."

Hailey pulled a small mirror from her purse and checked her makeup, then slanted a brief glance in Winn's direction. "I hope someone gives me goose bumps someday."

"It'll happen."

"I'm surprised I haven't been invited to a wedding."

Poppy just smiled and shrugged.

Hailey tilted her head, her gaze speculative. "Are you waiting for some kind of grand gesture?"

Poppy gave a little laugh. "If that's the case, I'll be waiting forever. Like I said before, Ben isn't a grand gesture kind of guy."

Bill hadn't been either, she recalled, then dismissed the thought. It wasn't fair to compare Ben to her ex.

Still, she couldn't help remembering the way Bill had proposed, traditional and straightforward. Though it had seemed romantic at the time, looking back it was almost as if getting married was a business proposition. He'd said all the right things, done the expected, but there had been little passion.

Poppy unexpectedly grinned. A grand gesture. A grand passion. Who knew she was such a romantic?

"Here you go." Cassidy set Hailey's glass of wine and Poppy's club soda on the table then dropped into a chair.

"Aren't you drinking?" Poppy asked.

"Are there elk in the elk refuge?" Cassidy reached into her mammoth purse and pulled out a can of beer. "I couldn't carry all three drinks so I had the bartender give me a can."

"I'm sorry," Poppy said. "One of us could have gone with you."

"And lose this great table? No way."

"Oh, my goodness." Poppy leaned to the side so she could see around Hailey. "Ben's parents just came in. I should go say hello."

She started to rise but Cassidy grabbed her arm. "Stay put, chickadee. The show is about to begin."

Poppy settled for giving John and Dori a wave. "I guess I can go over when there's a break."

"Good plan." Hailey took a sip of wine.

When Tripp appeared on stage, Poppy shifted her gaze to Hailey. "What's your brother—"

"Shush," Cassidy said. "It's starting."

"Tonight the Flying Crane is pleased to welcome to its stage, a first time performer. While he may be new to this, he's familiar to many of you. Give a big welcome to Dr. Benedict Campbell."

The glass of club soda slipped from Poppy's fingers. Hailey grabbed it before it tipped.

Ben entered from stage left and approached the microphone. Though he'd left the house in jeans and a sweater, he now wore a black tux that made him look tall, dark and sexy.

"There has to be some mistake," she said under her breath to Hailey. "Ben doesn't sing. He can't even carry a tune."

"Shh," Cassidy hissed.

"Before I get started," Ben began as Tripp slipped off stage. "I want to paint a picture for you."

Cassidy glanced at Hailey. "He's going to paint?"

Hailey rolled her eyes and motioned her quiet.

Ben's gray eyes were firmly focused on Poppy.

"I've been fortunate to have a thriving medical practice as well as family and friends who enrich my life. I wasn't unhappy. But something in my life was missing. Then, a little more than a year ago, I saw a beautiful woman with a beehive hairdo and a string of pearls across the room. At that moment, my life changed."

He held out a hand to Poppy.

She simply stared. Until Cassidy gave her chair a kick and Hailey hissed for her to stand. Seconds later she was on the stage beside him.

Ben took her hand, brought it to his lips for a kiss before continuing. "When I saw Poppy at that party, I knew she was something special. I knew she was the one I'd been waiting for my whole life. I know that she and I are meant to be together, forever."

He nodded toward the side of the stage and music flooded the bar.

It took Poppy a second to recognize it as Peaches and Herb's "I Pledge My Love." The wedding song from the eighties had experienced a brief resurgence in popularity several years ago.

It wasn't an easy song to sing, even by an experienced vocalist. Ben began in the wrong key but with the tenacity she'd come to expect and cherish in him, he forged ahead. The words "together forever" and "a lasting love" swirled through her head. Though his voice cracked and the hand holding the microphone shook slightly, the look of love in his eyes shone strong and steady.

Why had she not seen how much he cared before now? This man loved her. Not just a little, but with a depth of emotion that took her breath away. With this performance, he proclaimed those feelings to the world.

Slipping her arm through his, she began to sing the words that pledged her love to him...forever. The fact that her voice blended perfectly with his didn't surprise her. After all, they were a perfect match.

By the time the song ended, the audience was on its feet. Ben held up a hand to quiet the applause.

"For an encore—" He pulled a small velvet box from his pocket, flipped it open then dropped to one knee and took her hand.

"I love you more than life itself, Poppy. I believe we were meant to be together forever, that our love is lasting and pure. I pledge my love, my life to you. Will you do me the great honor of becoming my wife?"

Poppy stared into his face, familiar, known, increasingly beloved. All her doubts were gone, replaced with the knowledge that this was her man, the one she would love and who would love her, for the rest of their lives.

"Yes." Tears welled in her eyes. "Oh, yes."

He barely had time to slip the ring on her finger when her arms were around his neck and he was kissing her.

The crowd cheered.

"Perhaps we should sing to each other at our wedding?" Ben whispered against her mouth.

Poppy laughed with joy. Perhaps they should. Spontaneity had gotten them to this point.

And it couldn't have worked out any better.

Epilogue

Less than a week after a simple, but elegant, wedding at the Red Sands Hotel, John Andrew Campbell III made his appearance on a brisk fall day in early November. He had thick dark hair like his mother and a face that bore a striking resemblance to his handsome father.

Poppy gazed at the blue bundle nestled contentedly in Ben's arms. "Your dad seemed pleased by his namesake."

"Thrilled." Ben had seen the tears in his father's eyes. The same tears he'd seen him blink away last week when he and Poppy had spoken their wedding vows. "I think he liked it that we're going to call the baby Jack. That's what everyone called my grandfather."

"We have a lot to be thankful for this year." Poppy shifted her gaze from her son to Ben. Her heart overflowed with love. "To think one night led us here."

"One look. One night." Ben shifted his gaze between the baby boy squirming in his arms to the woman who'd made his life complete. "Now a lifetime of love ahead of us."

* * * * *

MILLS & BOON® *Book Club*

Join the Mills & Boon Book Club

Want to read more **Cherish**™ books?
We're offering you **2 more** absolutely **FREE!**

We'll also treat you to these fabulous extras:

- Exclusive offers and much more!

- FREE home delivery

- FREE books and gifts with our special rewards scheme

Get your free books now!

visit www.millsandboon.co.uk/bookclub
or call Customer Relations on 020 8288 2888

Wrap up warm this winter with Sarah Morgan...

Sleigh Bells in the Snow

Kayla Green loves business and hates Christmas.

So when Jackson O'Neil invites her to Snow Crystal Resort to discuss their business proposal... the last thing she's expecting is to stay for Christmas dinner. As the snowflakes continue to fall, will the woman who doesn't believe in the magic of Christmas finally fall under its spell...?

4th October

www.millsandboon.co.uk/sarahmorgan

Come home this Christmas to Fiona Harper

From the author of *Kiss Me Under the Mistletoe* comes a Christmas tale of family and fun. Two sisters are ready to swap their Christmases—the busy super-mum, Juliet, getting the chance to escape it all on an exotic Christmas getaway, whilst her glamorous work-obsessed sister, Gemma, is plunged headfirst into the family Christmas she always thought she'd hate.

www.millsandboon.co.uk

She's loved and lost — will she ever learn to open her heart again?

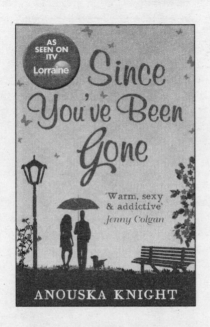

From the winner of ITV Lorraine's Racy Reads, Anouska Knight, comes a heart-warming tale of love, loss and confectionery.

'The perfect summer read — warm, sexy and addictive!'
—Jenny Colgan

For exclusive content visit:
www.millsandboon.co.uk/anouskaknight